PANDORA'S BOX

OSAMU DAZAI

Translated by
SHELLEY MARSHALL

CONTENTS

PANDORA'S BOX

Prologue	3
1. The Curtain Rises	5
2. The Health Dojo	12
3. Crickets	21
4. Death and Life	26
5. Mabo	33
6. Hygiene	43
7. Cosmos	48
8. My Little Sister	55
9. The Test	62
10. Stale Bread	74
11. Lipstick	82
12. Kashou Sensei	90
13. Take-san	101

GOODBYE

Prologue	113
1. A Change of Mind - 1	115
2. A Change of Mind - 2	117
3. The March - 1	119
4. The March - 2	121
5. The March - 3	123
6. The March - 4	125
7. The March - 5	127
8. Superhuman Strength - 1	129
9. Superhuman Strength - 2	131
10. Superhuman Strength - 3	133
11. Superhuman Strength - 4	135
12. The Cold War - 1	137
13. The Cold War - 2	139
Credits	141

PANDORA'S BOX

PROLOGUE

This novel takes the form of letters written to a close friend by a twenty-year-old man who is convalescing in a sanatorium called The Health Dojo. The few precedents of epistolary novels have been serialized in newspapers. Therefore, the first four or five sections may baffle the reader a bit, but the epistolary novel has a deepened sense of reality. For a long time, many authors in Japan and abroad have employed this form. The title *Pandora's Box* is the result of my intention to write the first part of this novel tomorrow, but there's nothing more I wish to say here.

This blunt prologue is discourteous, but a novel written by a man who gives this kind of curt greeting is surprisingly amusing.

(Fall 1945. Prologue by Dazai Osamu to the readers upon serialization in *Kahoku Shimpo*)

1

THE CURTAIN RISES

1

I'm not even a little melancholy. I received your encouraging letter, but I was confused by it and blushed from shame. Strangely, I can't calm down. Saying this may anger you, but old-fashioned came to mind when I read your letter. A new curtain has already been raised. Moreover, this curtain will rise on new experiences that none of our ancestors has ever had.

Are the old behaviors expected? They were mostly lies. Now, I have a disease of the chest, but am not worried at all. I've even forgotten what disease is. Not only disease, I've forgotten everything. I entered this Health Dojo because the war ended and life suddenly became precious. I'm here to regain my strength. Of course, I didn't come to somehow advance my station in life and didn't possess the touching, admirable devotion as a son to quickly recover to put my father at ease and to please my mother. I didn't come to this far-flung location out of desperation. Haven't we known for a long time that it's a mistake to attach meaning to each and every action of a person? Forced explanations often end in a distortion of lies. There are too many speculative games. And hasn't every idea been exhausted? I have entered The Health Dojo, but I want to say that it's for no reason at all. At some time on some day, a holy spirit crept into my chest, and tears cleansed my cheeks. After that, I cried alone often, and the strength drained from my body. My head felt cool and clear, and I became a different man. Until then, I had hidden this, but this time, I immediately told my mother, "I coughed up blood." My father selected The Health Dojo in the innards of these mountains for me. That's really all it was. Something happened at some time on some day? You probably understand this. That day. Noon on that day. That was the time I cried in a truly miraculous, divine voice and offered my apology.

Well, since that day, I felt as though I have been riding a huge, newly-built ship. But where is this ship going? Even I don't know. I'm still in a dreamscape. The ship is effortlessly leaving the shore. I have a vague premonition that it is heading in an uncharted virgin course that has never been experienced by anyone in the world. But now, only the huge new ship is welcomed and advances by yielding to the mercy of a sea lane in the heavens.

Don't get me wrong. I have not turned into a nihilist at the end of despair. Whatever the characteristics of the ship's departure, some kind of vague hope is always felt. That is the one human quality that has never changed. You probably know the old Greek myth of Pandora's Box. By simply opening a box that should not be opened, every imaginable evil, such as the pain of illness, sorrow, jealousy, greed, suspicion, treachery, hunger, and hatred, crept out and flew up to cover the sky. Since then, humanity has had to suffer in misery for all time. But it is said that a shining stone as small as a poppy seed remained in a corner of that box, and that stone is faintly inscribed with the word "Hope."

2

That was decided long ago. Despair is impossible in humans. They often are deceived by hope, but are also deceived by the notion of despair. Let me state this plainly. People fall into the depths of misery, but they grope for a ray of hope as they are tumbling down. Ever since Pandora's box, this fact has been prescribed by the gods of Olympus. People who speak of optimism or pessimism or act full of themselves and boast, especially those who are too ardent, are left on the shore. Our ships of this new age will steadily inch forward. There will be no bottlenecks. This motion mimics natural phototropism that transcends consciousness, resembling the spreading vines of a plant.

From now on, let's stop posturing with words to rashly censure and treat men as traitors. This only makes this unhappy world a little more dismal. Isn't an action like censuring another also negative and corrupt? Because we lost the war this time, we say that we would be happy if there were no politicians who are quick to fabricate deceptions to temporarily escape and who conspire to act with a modicum of ability. But this shallow, face-saving talk only occurs because things went wrong for Japan. I truly want people to be careful in the future. If this is repeated a second time, we may become despised throughout the world. We should become a more open and simple people without arrogance. This newly-built ship is already slipping out to sea.

I have harbored these harsh thoughts until now. As you know, last spring, I developed a high fever and came down with pneumonia around the time of the high school graduation. I couldn't take the college entrance exams because I was ill for three months. I somehow managed to get up and walk around, but a slight fever persisted and the doctor suspected pleurisy. While I was idly enjoying myself at home, this year's exam period came and went. Around that time, I lost interest in college. I could only see blackness before me, I didn't know what to do. It was no easy matter to prevent my father from criticizing my loafing around the house and my mother from seeing me as unworthy. You probably don't understand because you have never been a ronin, but it has been hell for me. During that time, I only weeded randomly. By pretending to be a farmer, I managed to keep up appearances. As you know, there's a field measuring a little less than an acre behind my house. For some reason, this field seemed to have had my name written on it for some time. But that's not the only reason, when I took one step onto that field, I remember feeling carefree, an escape from the pressures enveloping me. Over these last two years, I seemed to have become the ruler of this field.

I weeded and plowed the earth so much I couldn't feel my body. I also built supports for the tomatoes. Well, this may help to increase food production an iota. Each day I deceived myself, unlike you who could never deceive yourself. Anxiety was trapped in the depths of my heart, like a formation of black clouds I could not break free of. By living this way, what will my fortune be? There is nothing. Am I simply a sickly man? I was staggered by these thoughts. What should I do? I had no direction, nothing. I thought that this reckless life of mine was only a nuisance to others and devoid of meaning. This is quite hard to bear. A talented guy like you probably doesn't understand, but no thought in the world is worse than the realization that, "My life is a nuisance to others. I am useless."

3

But while I continue to be this spoiled-brat, distressed like some old-fashioned fool, you are a windmill turning round so fast in the world that you become invisible. I know almost nothing about the total destruction of the Nazis in Europe, the decisive battles in the Philippines and Okinawa in the East, the bombing of the interior of Japan by American warplanes, and the military tactics of the soldier in me. But, I carry a young, sensitive antenna inside of me. This antenna can be trusted. This antenna immediately senses depression and crisis in the country. There is no theory. It's only intuition. Around the beginning of summer this year, this young antenna of mine sensed the sounds of huge tidal bores that I have never experienced, and I trembled. But I had no plans, only confusion.

I worked hard but chaotically in the field. While sweating and moaning under the hot sun, I swung and turned a heavy hoe to dig up the earth in the field and planted sweet potato vines. I still can't understand why I continued to toil everyday in the field. Although my body was useless, out of what felt like desperation, I acted out a hateful, scathing punishment. There were days when each time I lowered the hoe, I would groan, "Die! Just die and end it! Die! Die and end it all!" I planted 600 sweet potato vines.

At dinner, my father would say, "Don't overwork in the field. You're being a little hard on your body." In the dead of night on the third day after that dinner, while dreaming, I had a severe coughing fit. There was some kind of rumbling in my chest. I suddenly realized that this was bad and woke up. I once read in some book that before you spit up blood, there is a rumbling in your chest. It came suddenly just as I lay down on my stomach. As my mouth filled with a foul smelling substance, I trotted off to the bathroom. As expected, there was blood. I stayed in the bathroom a long time, but no more blood came up. I snuck to the washroom and gargled with salt water, then washed my face and hands and went back to bed. I slept quietly so that I would breathe without coughing, and felt a curious indifference. I even felt like I had been waiting for that night for a long time. The words "heart's desire" came to mind.

Tomorrow, I thought, my silent work in the garden will continue. I have no choice. I am a person with no reason to live. I know my lot. Yes, it would be great to die one day sooner. Now, I will make better use of my body and be useful by increasing food production just a little, then I will bid farewell to this world. It would be good to lighten the burden on this country. That is my path to best serve my country as a useless invalid. I want to die soon.

The following morning, I woke up more than an hour earlier than usual. I quickly folded up my futon and went out to the field without eating. I chaotically worked that day in the field. Thinking about it now, it was like a hellish dream. Of course, I intended to die without telling a soul about my illness. Without anyone knowing, I would secretly deteriorate. These are probably rather depraved thoughts. That night, I snuck out and drank my fill of rationed rice alcohol from a rice bowl.

In the dead of night, I coughed up blood again. I awoke in a start, and when I lightly coughed two or three times, it came gushing up. This time, I didn't have time to run to the bathroom. I opened the glass door and jumped barefoot into the garden and threw up. My throat kept filling up, and it felt like blood was spraying out of my eyes and ears. It didn't stop until I threw up about two cups of blood. I don't know how much bloodstained earth I had turned over with a stick before the air-raid sirens sounded. Thinking about it, that was the final nighttime airstrike of that awful world in Japan. When I crept out of the air-raid shelter feeling numb, dawn had broken on the morning of August 15.

4

That day, however, I went out to the field. Hearing this, you are probably forcing a smile. But to me, there was nothing to laugh about. Actually, I felt that there was nothing else I could do. I had no alternatives. Shouldn't I be resolved to die as a peasant in my horribly confused final circumstance? My heart's desire was to collapse and die as a peasant in a field I tilled with my own hands. Yes, I wanted to die soon without any fuss. When I was splayed out on my back in a dense bean patch and grew faint passing through the pain of dizziness, chills, and covered in a clammy cold sweat, my mother came to get me. She told me to quickly wash my hands and feet and go to my father's sitting room. My mother always spoke with a faint smile on her lips and a solemn expression like a stranger.

I sat down in front of the radio in my father's sitting room, then at noon I cried in a heavenly voice while tears cleansed my cheeks. A mysterious light illuminated my body. I suddenly felt different as if I had stepped into another world or boarded a huge swaying ship, I was no longer what I had been.

I am not conceited about my realization of the oneness of life and death. But aren't life and death the same? Either one is equally hard. There are many poseurs among people who want a quick, unnatural death. My hardships until now were nothing more than the pains of embellishing my appearance. Are the old behaviors expected? Your letter had the phrase "sorrowful determination," but to me sorrowful seems like an expression of the handsome leading man in a corny play. This is not sorrow. That is already a false expression. The ship is slowly leaving the pier. There should always be a glint of hope when a ship sets sail. I am not depressed. I am not worried about this illness in my chest. I was actually confused by your letter filled with words of sympathy. With my mind blank, I intend to go forward by yielding to this ship. That day, I immediately confided in my mother. I was curiously calm when I unmasked myself.

"I coughed up blood last night and the night before."

I had no excuses. It was not because life suddenly became precious, but the forced pretense until yesterday had disappeared.

My father selected The Health Dojo for me. As you know, my father is a professor of mathematics. He's probably quite good at mathematical calculations, but he doesn't seem to have ever handled accounts of money. Because we have always been poor, I also never desired luxurious medical care. This simple Health Dojo is a good match for me, for that reason alone. I have no complaints. I should completely recover in six months. Since I arrived here, I haven't coughed up blood even once, and haven't even had bloody phlegm. I have forgotten all about the disease. The director of the Dojo said that "forgetting about the disease" is the fast track to complete recovery. That man is a bit eccentric. At any rate, he named a hospital for treating tuberculosis The Health Dojo. He probably did it to encourage more people to become patients under the special laws to fight disease that were enacted to address food and drug shortages during the war. This hospital is a queer place. Many amusing incidents happen here. I'll leisurely tell you about them the next time.

Please don't worry about me at all. And take care of yourself.

August 25, 1945

2

THE HEALTH DOJO

1

As promised, today I will tell you about The Health Dojo where I currently reside. It's about a one-hour bus ride from E City. You get off at a place called Little Plum Bridge to transfer to another bus. But it's not far from Little Plum Bridge to the Dojo, so it's faster to walk than to wait for the transfer bus. Since it's less than a mile, most people who come to the Dojo walk from there. If you go south from Little Plum Bridge on a paved prefectural road while keeping the mountains to your right, in about a mile, there is a small stone gate at the foot of the mountain. From there, you follow a row of pine trees, and near the end of the pine trees, you can see the roofs of two buildings. They constitute this peculiar sanatorium for tuberculosis dubbed The Health Dojo that is caring for me. The two buildings are the old building and the annex. The old building isn't much, but the annex is a stylish sunny building. One by one, the people who have acquired considerable training in the old building are moving to the annex. But none of this matters to me because I'm healthy and have been in the annex from the start. My room is the Sakura Room that is immediately to your right when you enter the front entrance of the Dojo. The hospital rooms are given strangely embarrassing cute names like the Verdure Room, the Swan Room, and the Sunflower Room.

The Sakura Room is a rectangular Western-style room, a little under 168 square feet. There are four sturdy wooden beds lined up so you can sleep with your head to the south. My bed is the furthest inside the room. Near the head of my bed is a large glass window outside of which is Otomegaike Pond (not much of a name), which is about one square mile. This pond is always clear and cool, and carp and goldfish can be seen swimming around. At least, I don't have any complaints about the placement of my bed. It may be the best spot. The bed is made of wood and is pretty big and doesn't have cheap springs. It's actually very practical with many drawers and shelves on both sides. Although I've surrounded myself with all my belongings, some drawers remain empty.

Now, I'll introduce you to my senior roommates.

Next to me is Ootsuki Matsuemon. His name sounds like that of a respectable, middle-aged man. They say he's a newspaperman from Tokyo. His wife died young so he lives with his teenage daughter. She was evacuated from Tokyo with him and lives in a house in the mountains near The Health Dojo. From time to time, she comes to visit her lonely father. The father is fairly sullen. Although he's usually a quiet man, he sometimes transforms into an obstinate man who is quick to anger. His personality seems to be honorable for the most part, but at times he seems a bit philosophical. I still don't really understand him. He has a splendid black mustache and is terribly near-sighted. Small bleary red eyes peer from behind his glasses. A bead of sweat always rests on the tip of his round nose and he's constantly wiping it off with a towel. As a result, the tip of his nose is red as if dripping blood. But if I shut my eyes and think about him, what comes to mind is dignity. He is probably an unexpectedly great man. His nickname is Echigo Lion. I don't know exactly why, but it feels perfect. Matsuemon doesn't seem to be bothered much by this nickname. They say he proposed his own nickname, but it baffles me.

2

Next to him is Kishita Seishichi, a plasterer. He's twenty-eight years old and still single. He is the best looking man at The Health Dojo. He is a fine specimen with his pale white skin, high pointed nose, and cool eyes. However, he walks a little tippy-toed while slightly swinging his hips. It would be nice if he'd just stop walking like that. Why does he walk like that? It may be because he's musical. He's incomprehensible. He appears to know various popular songs, but is particularly good at *Dodoitsu* poetry. I've already been forced to listen to five or six of them. Matsuemon closes his eyes and silently listens, but the poems make me uneasy. These stupid meaningless songs are about things like collecting a pile of money as big as Mount Fuji and spending 50 *sen* everyday. They are nothing more than a nuisance. And those *Monkukiri*-style Dodoitsu poems are terrible. Some of the songs seem to be lines from plays. Hey man, no one needs to hear any of that. But he doesn't sing more than two songs at any one time. If it seems he wants to continue singing any longer, Matsuemon won't allow it. When the two songs are over, Echigo Lion opens his eyes and says that's enough. Another thing, he touches his body. The meaning of touching the singer's body or the meaning of touching the listener's body is unclear. But Seishichi is not a bad guy. He seems to like haiku, and in the evening before bed, he recites various recent works to Matsuemon and seeks his thoughts, but Echigo does not respond. Seishichi becomes very despondent and quickly falls asleep. He seemed so pitiful at those times. Seishichi has a lot of respect for Echigo Lion. The nickname of this stylish man is Crazy Legs.

The next bed is occupied by Nishiwaki Kazuo. He's a postmaster or something. He's thirty-five years old. I like him the most. His quiet, petite wife sometimes visits. During those visits, they speak in whispers to each other. They have an air of secrecy. Both Crazy Legs and Echigo are respectful and try with all their might not to look. I think their intentions are good. Nishiwaki's nickname is Horsetail, probably because he's tall and lanky. He's not much to look at, but he is refined. He gives the impression of being a student.

His bashful, slight smile is charming. Sometimes, I think it would be great if he were my neighbor. But late at night, he moans in a weird voice, so it's probably better that he's not next to me. Now I have introduced you to my senior roommates. Next, I'll give a little report on the special therapies at the Dojo, beginning with the daily schedule.

6 am: Wake up
7 am: Breakfast
8 to 8:30 am: Bending and stretching exercises
8:30 to 9:30 am: Rubdown
9:30 to 10 am: Bending and stretching exercises
10 am: Rounds by the director (rounds only by the instructors on
Sundays)
10:30 to 11:30 am: Rubdown
12 pm: Lunch
1 to 2 pm: Lectures (Tranquility broadcasts on Sundays)
2 to 2:30 pm: Bending and stretching exercises
2:30 to 3:30 pm: Rubdown
3:30 to 4 pm: Bending and stretching exercises
4 to 4:30 pm: Nature
4:30 to 5:30 pm: Rubdown
6 pm: Dinner
7 to 7:30 pm: Bending and stretching exercises
7:30 to 8:30 pm: Rubdown
8:30 pm: Reports
9 pm: Bedtime

3

As I recently told you, because many hospitals burned down during the war, and quite a few hospitals were shut down because of shortages of goods and workers, many patients with tuberculosis who require long-term care, especially, those like us who aren't particularly rich, lose out on spots. Luckily, there were almost no attacks by enemy planes around here. Two or three powerful local philanthropists came forward and obtained the support of the local council to build an annex to the prefecture's sanatorium beside the mountain and summoned Dr. Tajima to build an independent sanatorium for tuberculosis that did not rely on raw materials. I gave you only a brief account of the daily schedule, but you probably understand that the normal activities at the sanatorium are very different. I plan to make you discard your notions of hospitals and patients.

The hospital administrator is called the director. The doctors from the assistant director on down are the instructors, the nurses are the assistants, and we, the patients, are the students. This all seems to be the invention of Director Tajima. After Dr. Tajima was invited to this sanatorium, the equipment was refurbished, and unique therapies were developed for the patients. The results were extremely good and seemed to have garnered the attention of the medical world. Dr. Tajima is completely bald and looks to be about fifty years old, but I've heard he's a single man in his thirties. He's a tall, thin man who slouches a little and doesn't laugh much. This bald man is fairly good looking; Dr. Tajima possesses elegant features with a cute oval face. He seems to have the usual, dismal, difficult-to-please nature of cats that is peculiar to bald men. He's a little scary. Every day at 10 am, the director makes rounds of the campus with the instructors and the assistants in tow. During that time, the entire Dojo becomes hushed. The students are incredibly meek before the director. They only whisper his nickname behind his back. It's Kiyomori, the villainous samurai who usurped political power.

Now, I'll fill in a few more details about the daily schedule at the Dojo. In short, the bending and stretching exercises are for the limbs and the abdominal muscles. Too many details will probably bore you, so I'll tell you just the important points. While splayed out on my back on my bed with my arms and legs spread wide as if sleeping, I begin by successively exercising my fingers followed by my wrists, then my arms. Next, I have to do a very difficult practice where I exhale to suck in my stomach to create a depression, then inhale to expand it. This is the most important bending and stretching exercise. Next come the leg exercises, the leg muscles are extended and loosened in various ways; this usually ends one round of bending and stretching. After one round is finished, I repeat from the hand exercises until the time limit of thirty minutes. This is done every single day, twice in the morning and three times in the afternoon as on the schedule, so it's not easy. According to known medical knowledge, these exercises are unbelievably dangerous to patients with tuberculosis, but it's probably a new therapy created because of shortages during the war. In this Dojo, patients who earnestly do these exercises seem to quickly recover.

Next, I'll tell you a little about the rubdown. This also appears to be unique to this Dojo. This is a role of the cheerful assistants at the Dojo.

4

The brush used in the rubdown is made of stiff animal bristles; the kind usually used when cutting hair. Fortunately, the bristles soften. So at first, it is painful to be rubbed by the brush, and your skin feels prickly here and there after being beaten up by the friction. But you get used to it in about a week.

At rubdown time, the always cheerful assistants split into groups and take turns giving the students rubdowns. A towel is folded and placed in a small basin containing water. The brush is pressed against the towel to soak up the water, then used in the rubdown. As a rule, most of the body is rubbed down. For your first week in the Dojo, only your arms and legs are rubbed down, but after that, your whole body. While you lay on one side, first your arm, then your leg, chest, and stomach are rubbed down. Then you turn over and they move to the arm, leg, chest, and stomach on the other side, and finally your back and waist. Once you get used to it, it feels good. Most of all, I can't describe what it feels like when your back is rubbed down. There are really skilled assistants and ones who are abysmal.

I'll tell you more about the assistants later.

You can consider life at the Dojo, both day and night, to be the two activities of the bending and stretching exercises and the rubdowns. Because shortages of materials didn't end after the war ended, for now, isn't this a good show of the spirit of fighting illness?

In addition, there are lectures at 1 pm, nature at 4 pm, and reports from 8:30 pm. The lectures are talks given by the director, the instructors, or prominent people from various fields who have come to inspect the Dojo. They take turns using the microphone. Their talks flow to our rooms through the loudspeakers placed strategically in the halls outside the rooms. We sit on our beds and listen in silence.

The lectures were suspended temporarily during the war because loudspeakers were useless due to power shortages. But after the war when restrictions on power use were eased a bit, they began again. At that time, the director resumed the lectures with themes like the history of scientific advances in Japan. Although they may be called intelligent lectures, they have an insipid tone and simply describe the hardships of our ancestors. Yesterday, the talk was about *The Beginnings of Dutch Studies* by Sugita Genpaku. Genpaku and his team were the first to study Western books, determined what would be a good way to translate them, and wrote "like a rudderless ship adrift on the vast sea, until reaching the point of being dismayed at being dismayed." It was actually good. My high school history teacher, Kiyama Ganmo, taught me about the hardships faced by Genpaku's team, but he left an entirely different impression. Ganmo only said vapid things like doesn't Genpaku's face seem to be terribly pockmarked.

The director's daily lectures are particularly enjoyable to me. On Sundays, he broadcasts records instead of giving a lecture. I don't care much for music, but listening to it once a week isn't bad. Between records, they broadcast a cappella singing by the assistants. Listening to the songs is more unsettling than enjoyable. But the other students seem to welcome the singing the most. Seishichi listens with his eyes narrowed. In my opinion, he is dying to broadcast the Monkukiri style of Dodoitsu.

5

Nature at 4 pm is a restful period. At this time, our body temperatures are the highest. The body is tired, you feel terribly irritable and become grim; it's quite distressing. They give us thirty minutes of free time to do as we please. But most of the students just quietly lie down on their beds during this period. At the Dojo, aside from sleeping at night, you aren't allowed to put bedding on your bed. During the day, you sleep on the bed in your nightclothes with no blankets, nothing, but it's refreshing when you get used to it and feels good. The reports at 8:30 pm are daily information about world affairs. A variety of news is reported in the nervous tones of the office staff on duty through those loudspeakers in the hall. At the Dojo, we are forbidden to read books, of course, as well as newspapers. Reading compulsively is probably bad for your body. While here, I have been flooded with crazy thoughts, but I only firmly believe in the new ship setting sail, living simply, and playing. I think that's okay.

I have so little time to write you and am at a loss. Usually after meals, I quickly take out my writing pad, but there's so much I want to write. It took me two days to write this letter. As I gradually become accustomed to life at the Dojo, I'll probably use these short breaks more adeptly. I have become a very optimistic scholar about everything. I have not a worry in the world. I have forgotten them all.

I must make one more introduction, my nickname at the Dojo is Skylark. Now, that name is lackluster. My full name is Koshiba Risuke, but people hear Kohibare, a small skylark, so I'm Hibari, Skylark, and that seems to be how I got this nickname. It's not very distinctive. Firstly, it's horrible, as well as embarrassing and not suited to me. But I have become magnanimous about these kinds of things and cheerfully respond even to people who call out Skylark. Do you understand? I have been Koshiba for a long time. Now, there is a skylark in this Health Dojo. This one is chirping loudly and noisily. So from now on, please read my letters with this in mind. I'm a frivolous guy. Please stop frowning.

"Skylark," shrieks an assistant from outside my window.

"What?" I calmly respond.

"Ya doin' it?"

"I'm doin' it."

"Keep it up."

"I got it."

Do you understand this exchange? This is the greeting at the Dojo. The assistants and the students have this exchange whenever they pass each other in the halls. I don't know when this started. Do you think the director agreed to this? This is, no doubt, an invention of the assistants. Resilience and toughness, a little like boys, seem to be the shared disposition of the nurses. The providers of sarcastic nicknames to everyone, the director, the instructors, the students, and the staff, are the assistants. They're always a little sly. I have closely observed the assistants. I'll tell you more about them in my next letter.

This concludes my sketch of the Dojo. Goodbye for now.

September 3

3

CRICKETS

1

Greetings,

I am at your service. September has come and so much has changed. The wind is chilly like it skimmed the pond's surface. The insect sounds have become piercing. I'm not a poet like you and don't have any particular feeling like my heart is about to break. Last night, however, a young assistant stood alone near the pond below my window, looked at me and laughingly said, "Tell Horsetail, the crickets are chirping."

When I heard those words, I realized that fall deeply penetrates these people and felt a little suffocated. From the beginning, this assistant seemed to favor my roommate Nishiwaki Horsetail.

When I replied, "Horsetail's not here. He went to the office a few minutes ago," she quickly became ill-tempered and rudely responded with the odd counterattack of, "Oh, that's okay. Skylark, you hate crickets, don't you?" I didn't understand where that came from and was bewildered.

There are many things I don't understand about this young

assistant. From the beginning, I've been the most wary of her. Her nickname is Mabo, the kid Ma.

Today, I'll describe the assistants' nicknames. In the last letter, I told you that these assistants were a sly bunch and gave sarcastic nicknames to one and all. Not to be defeated, the students gave nicknames to all of the assistants. We seem to be tied. But the nicknames invented by the students are kind to the women and are somewhat gentle. Miura Masako is Mabo. This is obvious. Takenaka Shizuko is Take-san, the least imaginative. Very commonplace. And the assistant who wears glasses, favors a telescope goldfish, and is reserved becomes Goldfish. The one who is thin becomes bug-eyed Sardine. The one with a wobegone look is Spiced Tea. She's probably nice, but is a little reserved. The one who is pretty homely, but has a ghastly permanent wave, eyelids painted red, and caked on grotesque make-up is Peahen. She's probably called Peahen to mock her, but she is quite proud of her nickname. She seems to say with utter confidence, "Yes, I am Peahen." I don't hear a shred of sarcasm. Me, I would have called her Heavenly Maiden. "Don't you think I'm the Heavenly Maiden?" Other names are Reindeer, Cricket, Detective, and Onion, they're all pretty bland. Another is named Heatstroke. I think this one was cleverly named. This assistant has a wide face and bright glowing red cheeks that definitely remind you of an ogre's face. As you would expect, she's reserved and elusive, like the devil succumbing to heatstroke, so she is Heatstroke. This idea is elegant.

"Heatstroke."

"What?" she answers decisively.

"Keep it up."

"I got it," she responds energetically.

I can't match Heatstroke's tenacity. Not just her, all the assistants here have a bit of a wild side, but they're all really kind, good people.

2

The most popular assistant among the students is Take-san,

Takenaka Shizuko. She's not beautiful, but is imposing, about 5 feet, 2 inches, nice boobs, and a darkish complexion. She's about twenty-five or twenty-six years old. But her distinctive feature is her smiling face. This may be why she is the most popular assistant. She has a refreshing feeling with her large eyes whose corners raise up and narrow like needles when she laughs and exposes her bright white teeth. The white nurse's uniform suits her well because she is big. Another source of her popularity may be her diligence. "She's the best wife in Japan," remarked Crazy Legs on her finesse in cleverly and rapidly finishing her work. However, you may view the other assistants chatting idly with the students or teaching each other popular songs during rubdowns in a positive light as being congenial, or in a negative light as being lackadaisical. If a student initiates a conversation about anything, only Take-san will just ambiguously nod in agreement with a slight smile and continue the rubdown with her rhythmic manual technique. Her rubdowns are neither too strong nor too weak, and are by far the most skillful. She's careful, always silent with a small, but bright smile, and never complains and never engages in tedious small talk. She seems to stand apart from the other assistants. This slightly reserved dignity of solitude may be her most charming feature to the students. At any rate, she's very popular. As Echigo Lion has said, "the mother of that child is most surely a reliable woman." So it seems. Take-san seems to hail from Osaka, and remnants of the Kansai dialect linger in her speech. That is an incredibly good asset as far as the students are concerned. For a long time, when I saw a woman with a fine body, it would remind me of a sea bream, the prized fish. I would wryly smile and only feel sorry for her and lose all interest in her. I prefer cuteness over dignity in a woman. Now, Mabo is small and cute. My interest is captured by the somewhat enigmatic Mabo.

Mabo is eighteen years old. She promptly came here after leaving a public girl's high school in Tokyo. She has a round face with a pale, white complexion and large, slightly droopy eyes with double eyelids and long eyelashes. Those eyes always have a look of surprise, which causes creases to form on her forehead making her narrow forehead even narrower. Her laugh is wild and exposes a sparkling gold-capped tooth. Looking as if she were dying to laugh with those huge eyes saying What?, she thrusts her head forward into any conversation, and instantly bursts out laughing while slouching forward, patting her stomach, and choking on her laughs. Her round button nose rises high. Her thin lower lip protrudes a little below her upper lip. She's no beauty, but she is terribly cute. She doesn't work particularly hard and gives a horrible rubdown. But she somehow bursts with cuteness and is no less popular than Take-san.

3

That reminds me. The guys here are funny. They constantly give mocking nicknames to girls they have no interest in, like Heatstroke and Spiced Tea, but to someone nice, they can't think of any nickname and can only come up with uninteresting names like Take-san and Mabo. Oh well, today, I stupidly only have stories about women. Why don't I want to talk about anything else today? Yesterday, I was charmed by Mabo's lovely words, "Tell Horsetail, the crickets are chirping," and may still be charmed. Despite Mabo's demented laugh, she may actually be an uncommonly sad girl. Doesn't a person who laughs a lot also cry a lot? When I think about Mabo, I feel strange. It's unbearable because evidently Mabo wants to talk with Nishiwaki Horsetail. I'm hastily writing this letter right after plowing through lunch. I can clearly hear Mabo's shrill, boisterous laughing voice mixed in with the laughter of the students coming from the Swan Room next door. What is that racket about? Disgraceful. Idiots. Today, I'm feeling a little out of sorts. There are a lot of things I want to write about, but the laughter next door makes me uneasy and I can no longer write. I'll rest a while.

Finally, the racket has subsided, so I'll write a little more. Well, I don't understand Mabo very well. There's no particular reason, but seventeen and eighteen year-old girls are all probably like that. You never find a personality that is all good or all bad. Every time I meet her echoes the first time Sugita Genpaku opened a book in a Western language. It's a bit of an exaggeration to say that I am "like a rudderless ship adrift on the vast sea, until reaching the point of being dismayed at being dismayed," but the truth is I falter a bit. I'm quite anxious. Now, I've stopped writing the letter because of those laughing voices, and have thrown my pen aside and myself into bed. I can't calm down and can no longer bear it. While I was lying in bed, I pointedly complained to Matsuemon, who's next to me,

"Isn't Mabo loud?"

Matsuemon calmly sitting cross-legged on his bed agreed while picking his teeth with a toothpick, he then slowly wiped the sweat from his nose with a towel and said, "The mother of that child is bad."

Everything is the mother's fault.

Mabo was probably raised by an evil stepmother. Although cheerful, she has an air of sadness. Today, I really like Mabo.

"Tell Horsetail, the crickets are chirping,"

Since that time, I've felt very strange. A trifling woman.

September 7

4

———————

DEATH AND LIFE

1

Please excuse my weird letter yesterday. As the seasons turn, everything seems brand new, and I yearn for love. I like her. I really like her. I am going completely berserk. No, I don't like her that much. I blame it all on the start of fall. Recently, I've come to resemble a noisy, loud, chattering skylark and twitter like a birdbrain. But, I don't hate myself for it or feel a deep, bitter regret. Initially, I thought that the elimination of that feeling of hatred was a mystery, but it's not a mystery at all. Didn't I intend to become an entirely different man? I have become the New Man. So far, my greatest joy is not feeling self-hatred or regret. I think that's a good thing. Now, as the New Man, I possess a refreshing self-confidence. During the six months I'll be at the Dojo, I will think of nothing and be given the precious way to live naively and playfully. The skylark sings. Spring water flows. I live transparently and with lightness!

In my letter yesterday, I praised Mabo highly, but I want to lower that a bit. An unusual incident occurred. I will soon fill in the omissions of my previous letter. Don't laugh at the singing skylark, the flowing spring water, and this birdbrain.

Mabo gave me my rubdown this morning. It's been a long time. Too bad Mabo's rubdowns are lousy. The rubdowns she gives to Horsetail are probably done with care, but mine are always sloppy and thoughtless. Perhaps, Mabo thinks nothing more of me than a pebble on the side of the road. Oh well. But to me, Mabo is not a mere pebble. During a rubdown given by her, I tense up, can hardly breathe, and can barely speak. Worst of all, I can't even joke. When I tell a joke, my voice gets caught in my throat and almost nothing comes out. As a result, I look sullen and end up sulking. This probably makes Mabo uncomfortable, so she doesn't laugh at all and says little only during my rubdowns. This morning's rubdown was agonizingly strained. Particularly since she said, "Tell Horsetail, the crickets are chirping," I immediately became anxious. Right after I wrote that letter telling you that I really liked Mabo, I don't really understand it, but the awkwardness I felt became unbearable. While rubbing my back, Mabo unexpectedly whispered,

"Skylark's the best."

I wasn't happy at all. I thought she hated saying that. This fake compliment was proof that Mabo thinks I'm not sensible. If she really thought I were the best, she wouldn't say it so freely and plainly. I'm well aware of those kinds of subtleties. I said nothing. Then again in a quiet voice, she said, "I have a problem." Now that surprised me. I would have said something awful, but I was tired.

"The crickets are chirping" has a totally negative connotation. I suspect she may be an imbecile. For some time, I've believed that laugh of hers was idiotic, but my spirits lifted thinking that it may be genuine.

"What sort of problem could you possibly have?" I managed to ask in a mocking tone.

2

She didn't answer, then lightly sniffled. When I looked at her from the corner of my eyes...oh no...she was crying. I was dumbfounded. Just like I wrote in yesterday's letter, "Isn't a person who laughs a lot, one who cries a lot?" When I see this disappointing realization of my dumbass prediction, I am disheartened and disgusted with myself. This is ridiculous.

"It's Horsetail's leaving the Dojo," I said jokingly. But this is an actual rumor. I heard that for family reasons, Horsetail has to return to the hospital near his home in Hokkaido.

"Stop fooling around."

She quickly stood up, then without finishing the rubdown, grabbed the metal basin, and hurriedly left the room. I confess I looked at her figure as she left, and my heart beat a little faster. In my conceit, I didn't think she had any problem with me. At the very least, the bubbly Mabo letting a man see her cry real tears and then departing in anger may be a big deal. Perhaps, no matter how much I suppressed it, a little conceit was able to escape, and the earlier contempt was swept away. I often thought Mabo was adorable. I felt like screaming. I lay in bed swinging both arms around. Then I got it. I suddenly understood the meaning of Mabo's tears. At that time, Goldfish, who was rubbing down Echigo Lion, nonchalantly told me, "She was reprimanded. Last night, Take-san told her that she gets too carried away and boisterous."

Take-san supervises the assistants, so she's probably allowed to reprimand any of them. I understood everything. I got it. I completely understood. That's it! She was reprimanded by her supervisor. How dreadful. I was mortified. My pathetic conceit made me feel like Goldfish, Echigo Lion, and everyone else could see right through me and were smiling out of pity. This time, the New Man was stunned into silence. I got it. I understood it all. I intend to make a clean break from Mabo. The New Man is decisive. The New Man has no regrets. From now on, I intend to completely ignore Mabo. She is a cat, actually, a trivial woman. I feel like laughing to myself, "Ah! Ha ha ha!"

At noon, Take-san brought my tray. Usually, she quickly leaves, but today she set the tray on the small desk beside my bed. She then stretched and gazed out the window, then took two or three steps toward it. She placed both hands on the sill and silently stood with her back to me. She seemed to be looking at the pond in the garden. I sat on my bed and immediately started eating. The New Man does not complain about side dishes. The day's side dishes were dried sardines and boiled pumpkin. I ate the sardines piece by piece beginning at the head. I chewed each piece methodically and thoroughly to capture all of the nourishment.

"Skylark," said Take-san in a voiceless whisper. When I looked up, Take-san had turned around with both hands behind her back and was leaning against the window facing me. With her characteristic faint smile, in a very soft voice like she was only breathing, asked, "Was Mabo crying?"

3

"Yeah," I answered in my usual voice, "She said, 'I have a problem.'" I must chew methodically and thoroughly to create healthy blood.

"Horrible," said Take-san quietly while frowning.

"I don't know anything about it."

The New Man is candid. He has no interest in women's problems.

"I'm a little worried," she said grinning, then blushed.

I was a little flustered and swallowed an unchewed bite.

"Eat everything," she quickly said in a low voice as she passed in front of me and left the room.

Unintentionally, my words were sharp. What is this? How arrogant. How negligent. Why did you feel that way and didn't like it very much? Aren't you the supervisor? I didn't reprimand anyone, and I'm not worried. I was disgusted. Isn't Take-san the one who needs to be in control? But when she came with my third serving of rice, this time, I blushed. The rice bowl was too full. I always expect a light third serving, one I can finish, but today the third serving was as big as the first and a little rice remained at the bottom of the small bowl. I didn't know what to do. I hate this type of kindness. This form of kindness doesn't taste so good. This tasteless rice will become neither blood nor meat. It will become nothing. It's futile. Echigo Lion would probably say, "Take-san's mother is without a doubt a lady from the old school."

I only ate three light servings as always, and the later serving of my favorite remained untouched. Soon a composed Take-san came to retrieve the tray. I casually said, "I left some rice."

Take-san didn't look at me, but lifted the lid to peek into the bowl.

"Horrible child," she said almost inaudibly and took the tray. Expressionless, she left the room as if nothing had happened.

She said "horrible" in her usual tone. It probably didn't mean anything, but a woman saying "horrible" to me doesn't make me happy. In fact, it's awful. The old me would have slugged Take-san. Why am I horrible? Aren't you the horrible one? In the old days, the maid was expected to stealthily put rice in your favorite apprentice bowl, but that was an imbecilic, improper affection. Just wretched. Don't be ridiculous. I'm proud of myself as a New Man. Even with less rice, if I cheerfully chewed my food, I would extract all of the nutrition. I thought Take-san was a more dependable person, but women are useless after all. Usually, when this kind of folly is acted out by what seems to be clever, nonchalant behavior, the folly becomes more apparent and dirty. It's a pitiful situation. Take-san needs to get a grip.

In contrast, if this were Mabo acting out any failure, her cuteness and loveliness would probably be magnified. Blunders by a fine woman are distressing. I'm using the break after lunch to write this, but the loudspeaker in the hall snapped on and ordered all of the students in the annex to immediately assemble at the balcony of the annex.

4

I put away my letter and went to the balcony on the second floor to see what was happening. A young student named Narusawa Itoko, who lived in the old building, died late last night, and everyone gathered together for her silent departure. The strained faces of the twenty-three male and six female students of the annex could be seen lined up in four rows resembling a military formation to await the departure of her casket. The white cloth wrapped around Narusawa-san's casket exquisitely reflected the autumn light. While her relatives watched, the casket was slowly lowered to the asphalt surface of the slightly sloping street that cut through the pine trees to the old building. I could see a woman who appeared to be her mother crying and dabbing her eyes with a handkerchief as she walked. The group of instructors and assistants dressed in white followed with their heads bowed.

This is a good thing, I thought. People depend on death to be complete. While alive, they are all incomplete. Insects and small birds are perfect while they are alive, but are mere carcasses as soon as they die. They are neither complete nor incomplete, they merely return to nothing. By comparison, people are the exact opposite. The paradox of people becoming the most human because they will die seems to be valid. Narusawa-san's fight against illness, her death, the beautiful cloth symbolizing innocence that enveloped her, and now, her journey down the sloping road while being concealed by and revealed through the rows of pine trees are the most solemn, the most concrete, and the most eloquent proclamation of the existence of this young soul. We can never forget Narusawa-san. I discreetly directed my hands held together in prayer toward the luminous white cloth.

Don't misunderstand me. Although I said that death is good, I don't devalue or lightly view a person's life, and I surely am not a sentimental, apathetic "glorifier of death." We all live a sheet of paper away from death, so we shouldn't be surprised by death. Never forget this point.

Looking at what I've written so far in this letter, in this era of resentment, reflection, and gloom in Japan, you have surely felt indignant about the easy-going, overly cheerful air surrounding me. That's understandable. However, I am not a fool. Naturally, I'm not laughing wildly from morning 'til night. I hear a variety of news during the 8:30 report every evening. Although I sleep quietly covered by a blanket, there are nights when I lie awake. But I don't want to state the obvious to you. We are patients with tuberculosis. There are people who may cough up blood tonight and end up like

Narusawa-san. The source of our laughter is the small stone that tumbled into a corner of Pandora's box.

The smile of one flower permeates those who live next to death more than the problem of life and death. We are enticed by the faint scent of that flower to ride on that unfathomably large ship and yield to drifting on this sea lane in the heavens. I don't know what kind of island is the destination of this so-called Ship of Providence. However, we must believe in this voyage. I've come to feel that living or dying is not the key that determines a person's happiness or sorrow. The dead are complete, and the living stand on the deck of the ship about to set sail with their hands together. The ship glides away from the pier.

"Death is a good thing."

Does this mirror the calm of an experienced voyager? The New Man is unsentimental toward death and life.

September 8

5

MABO

1

I immediately read your reply with a tinge of nostalgia. My writing "Death is a good thing" was dangerous because it could easily be misinterpreted. I was so happy that you understood everything I wrote and accurately interpreted my feelings. I feel compelled to ponder the times. People of the previous age probably couldn't understand this serene attitude toward death at all. I suffered when I read the words in your letter, "Today's youth live next to death. This is not limited to victims of the atomic bombs. Our lives have been given to others. Our lives are not our own. So we can devote ourselves without reserve and without any hesitation to that so-called Ship of Providence. This is the new form of courage for a new century. Long ago on the ship, it was determined that we are an inch of plank away from death. Mysteriously, however, we don't care."

First, I must apologize for spewing my rage by saying your first letter felt old-fashioned. I don't mean that we are wasting our lives. But we should not sink vainly into sentimentality about or become afraid of death. As proof, after seeing off Narusawa Itoko's brilliant casket wrapped in white cloth, I completely forgot about Mabo and Take-san. I lay on my bed in a pure state of mind elevated like today's autumn sky and listened to the customary greetings between the students and assistants in the hall.

"Ya doin' it?"

"I'm doin' it."

"Keep it up."

"I got it."

They didn't have the usual half-joking tone, but somehow sounded like they were filled with conviction. In contrast to the students with their strained, meek shouts, I felt extremely healthy. If my words seem a little affected, it's because the entire Dojo felt sacred the entire day. I believed. Death never withers a person's feelings.

The pitiful people of an older era could only understand these feelings of ours as childish bravado or hopelessness at the end of despair. Don't you feel that few people clearly understand the passions in both the old and the new eras? We believe that life is light like a feather. But this doesn't mean that life is wasted. We love life as something light as a feather. That feather gently flies far, far away. While the adults continue to loudly debate patriotism and responsibility for the war, we'll leave them behind and immediately depart under the orders of an exalted gentleman. I truly feel that these are the characteristics of the new Japan.

I developed a surprising theory after Narusawa Itoko's death, however, this kind of theory is not my specialty. The New Man yields in silence to the newly built ship and is comfortable with life on the mysteriously bright ship. How about a story about another woman?

2

You really stood up for Take-san in your letter. If you like her that much, you should send a letter directly to her. No, even better, you should meet her. If you have the time, come to the Dojo not to visit me, but to see Take-san. If you see her, you'll be disappointed.

Nonetheless, she's a formidable woman. Her arms are probably stronger than yours. According to your letter, you said that Mabo's crying was of no consequence, but that Take-san saying, "I'm a little worried," was a major incident. I had to think about that. You wanted me to have the ridiculous conceit that her saying, "I'm a little worried," about Mabo coming to me with her troubles and crying was proof that Take-san has been interested in me for some time. But I don't sense the tiniest trace of that feeling, nothing. Take-san is a big girl with zero sex appeal. She's the type of person who's always busy working and has no time for thinking about anything other than work. She has the stress of the responsibility as the supervisor of the assistants and diligently works. Take-san reprimanded Mabo that evening. I heard from some of the assistants that Mabo was dejected and crying after being reprimanded. Perhaps, Take-san should reflect on her method of reprimanding. Maybe, it's a little too strong, and she should be concerned. I think that saying "I'm a little worried" was incredibly unsophisticated in this case, but was the soundest idea. I am certain of that. A woman thinks solely about her position. The New Man has not the slightest conceit about women and is unpopular among them. He is candid.

Take-san blushed when she said, "I'm a little worried," but that meant she was worried about having reprimanded Mabo. It was nothing more than the sudden awareness that those rapidly uttered words had an unexpectedly strange echo and her slight confusion made her blush. This is quite trivial. To unravel all of the factors on that day, Mabo crying to me, the worry, or the favor of a bowl of rice, one crucial fact must be considered. That is Narusawa Itoko's death. Narusawa-san died that night. After that, the scolding of the cheerful Mabo was revealed. The assistants are young women like Narusawa Itoko. They were probably deeply shocked. The old-fashioned emotions still seem to linger in women. Aren't the sadness and confusion and the charity of a bowl of rice manifestations of strange emotions? On that day, in particular, all of the factors seemed to have been bound to Narusawa Itoko's death. Neither Mabo nor Take-san has any special intentions for me. I'm not joking.

Well, do you understand? You appear to like Take-san. Just once, you should visit the Dojo and see the real thing. I think it's good that rather than Take-san, Mabo has the new sensibility, but you seem to dislike Mabo. That's something you should reconsider. Mabo does have a few good points. The day before yesterday, Mabo let me see her good-natured side, and I promptly reassessed her. Today, I'll tell you about one incident. You'll definitely come to like Mabo.

3

The day before yesterday, my roommate Nishiwaki Horsetail finally left the Dojo because of family circumstances. Mabo had the day off, so she promised to see Horsetail off to E City. Beginning the day before, the students made great fun of Mabo. From everywhere came persistent requests for souvenirs, they were clever, light-hearted, and good humored. Early morning on that day, Mabo wearing her *Monpe* work pants, made in Kurume-gasuri, joyfully set off following Horsetail. As we began the bending and stretching exercises that afternoon around three, she returned grinning and laughing, not like someone who had just parted from a dear friend. She walked around from room to room handing out the promised souvenirs to the students.

In these times of labor shortages, even the daughters from fairly well-off families have had to leave home to work. Mabo seems to be from that class and work is partly for fun. As a result, her warm reputation and unabating generosity are sources of her popularity among the students. Souvenirs these days are an extravagance. Where and under what circumstances did she get the souvenirs? They were toy mirrors about 1 to 2 inches tall? A photograph of a movie actress was pasted on the back. Years ago, these things were freely given out as gifts at neighborhood candy stores. Now, you have to buy them, and they're probably not cheap. She returned after buying the stock of several dozen from a candy store or a toy store somewhere. They are definitely souvenirs Mabo would dream up. The students were excited about the appealing pictures of the movie actress on the back. Crazy Legs received one, too. Because I hate the idea of receiving a gift from a woman, from the start, I didn't push for a souvenir, and thought that the favor of the same pocket mirror as the others was uncreative. Mabo came to our room and handed a mirror to Crazy Legs.

"Crazy Legs do you know who this actress is?"

"Nope, but she's a beauty. Mabo, she sort of looks like you, doesn't she?"

"Oh no...Isn't she Danielle Darrieux?"

"An American?"

"No French. She used to be very popular in Tokyo. Do you know her?"

"No, I don't. France, wherever, here, take it back. I'm not interested in a hairy foreigner. You could at least replace it with the photo of a Japanese actress. If you do, then I'll accept it. Why don't you give this to Oshiba Skylark over there."

"You talk too much. I have a special one only for you. It's not for Skylark. He's too mean."

"Who is she? Give it to me. Dani...?"

"Danielle. Danielle Darrieux."

While listening to their conversation, I continued the bending and stretching exercises without smiling, but it wasn't fun at all. Does Mabo dislike me that much? Of course, I didn't think she liked me, but it never occurred to me that she disliked me, and only me, that much. Even though my standing was at its lowest, there is yet another bottom below the bottom. After all, don't people live intoxicated by illusions about themselves? Reality is harsh. What makes me so awful? The next time, I want to seriously ask Mabo why. My chance would come surprisingly soon.

4

A little after 4 pm that day during nature time, I was lying on my bed gazing lazily out the window and saw Mabo, who had changed into her white uniform, suddenly emerge from the garden carrying laundry. Without thinking, I stood up and leaned halfway out the window.

"Mabo," I softly called.

Mabo turned and laughed when she saw me.

"May I please have a souvenir?" I asked.

She didn't answer immediately and quickly spun completely around. She seemed aware of her surroundings and who was watching. It was rest time, and the Dojo was hushed. Mabo laughed stiffly. She placed her palms beside her mouth and communicated without making a sound by forming the words with her mouth. I understood instantly.

"LA-TER O-KAY," she said.

Although I got it immediately, I deliberately formed my mouth into the same shapes, "LA-TER?" Again, she said each syllable separated by a pause. "LA-TER O-KAY." Next, she moved her hands together to signal secrecy. She bobbed slightly as she shrugged laughing and trotted off to the annex.

"Later okay. Well, fear is worse than reality." This made my heart flutter as I fell into bed. There is no need to explain my delight. I'll leave it to your imagination.

During last night's rubdown, I received the "later okay" souvenir from Mabo. From time to time beginning yesterday morning, Mabo drifted down the hall with purpose, looking like something was hidden under her apron. I thought that maybe the souvenir for me was concealed there. I brazenly outstretched my hand to her. When met with the counterattack, "Do you need something?" my face took on a look of indifference because of great humiliation. That was the gift for me.

For the 7:30 pm rubdown last night, it was Mabo's turn to give me a rubdown after about a week's absence. Carrying the metal basin in her left hand and hiding something in her right hand under her apron, Mabo came grinning and crouched down beside my bed.

"Meany. You didn't come to get it. I waited in the hall a couple of times since this morning."

She opened the drawer of my bed, quickly slid in the object from beneath her apron and shut the drawer.

"Don't say a thing. Not a word to anyone."

I slightly nodded two or three times while lying down. She began the rubdown.

"It's been a while Skylark. My number never came up. I couldn't figure out how to pass your souvenir to you."

I brought my hands close to my neck and mimed tying to silently ask if it were a necktie?

"No," she said laughing while her bottom lip jutted out, and in a soft voice added, "Dummy."

In fact, I am stupid. I don't even own a suit. A necktie. What an odd guess. Ludicrous. Maybe, I subconsciously associated the necktie with those small pocket mirrors.

5

Next, I mimed writing with my right hand to ask whether it was a fountain pen. In reality, I'm a selfish guy. My fountain pen is in pretty bad shape and I wanted a new one, so it suddenly came out. I'm disgusted with my real intentions and boldness.

"Nope," said Mabo shaking her head. I was out of ideas.

"It may be a little plain, but don't give it away. There was only one left in the store. It may not be first class, but walk around carrying it when you leave this place. You're a gentleman, Skylark, so you need one."

I was stumped. What was it, a walking stick?

"Well, thanks," I said while turning over.

"What are you saying? What a dope, this guy. Hurry up and get well, and leave."

"I'll do you a big favor. Yes, I'll die right here."

"What! Not that. There are people who will cry."

"Mabo?"

"You sure think a lot of yourself. Is there anyone who would cry? There's not much reason to cry."

"That's what I thought."

"I wouldn't cry. How many people would cry for Skylark?"

Mabo asked, then after a little thought, she said, "Three...no...four people."

"Crying is meaningless."

"No, there is meaning," she insisted and leaned down placing her mouth close to my ear.

"Maybe...Take-san...Goldfish...Onion...Heatstroke?" she named each one as she counted them with her fingers.

"Wow!" she said laughing.

"Heatstroke can cry?" I joked.

That night's rubdown was fun. I wasn't hard on Mabo like before. Now, I'm calm as if looking down at everyone from a high place and can joke around. Maybe, it's because I've simply tossed aside the stifling desire of wanting a woman to like me over this past half a month. It's a mystery to me too, but my few complaints have disappeared, and I've had fun. Liking and being liked seem like the leaves of a tree rustling in the May winds. My egotism is gone. The New Man leaps up.

After the rubdowns ended that night, we heard over the loud-speakers during the report that the American Occupation Army Forces had finally reached this area. I searched the drawers of my bed, took out, and unwrapped Mabo's gift.

It was a small package, about a 3½-inch square. Inside was a cigarette case. "Walk around carrying it when you leave this place. You're a gentleman, Skylark, so you need one." I now understood the meaning of those words that were incomprehensible to me just a short time ago.

When I took the case out of the box and inspected it, turning it over and over, I was hit by a wave of sadness. I am unhappy, and not only the world news is to blame.

6

The silver case is flat, probably made of stainless steel or a metal like the chrome used to make cake knives. A rose vine design is drawn on the lid in tangled thin black lines. The edges of the lid are decorated with what seems to be russet-colored enamel. It would be fine without the enamel, but is "a little plain" as Mabo said and "may not be first class" with this pointless enamel decoration. But, after all, Mabo did buy this for me, and I should cherish it.

But this is no fun. I can't say I received it. I'm actually a little unhappy. This is the first time I got a gift from an unrelated woman. I shouldn't feel weighed down by it, but I feel wretched and buried the case in the depths of my drawer. I want to forget about it immediately.

I'm also a little embarrassed and don't know what to do with the case. I want to use this kind of situation to understand Mabo's goodness, even a little. Then your letter came. Maybe I should re-evaluate Mabo. At any rate, Take-san is great. I want to hear your thoughts.

Today, Stale Bread, who had been living next door in the Swan Room, moved to Horsetail's bed. His name is Sukawa Goro, and he's twenty-six years old. Stale Bread appears to be a law student and a very popular guy. He has thick, deep black eyebrows and wears [Harold] Lloyd glasses with round rims propped on his aquiline nose, but something about him is off. Nevertheless, he does put the assistants in a tizzy. As much as the men seem to dislike him, the women like him. The Sakura Room has developed an unusual, awkward tension with the arrival of Stale Bread. Crazy Legs already considered Stale Bread to be an enemy. During the rubdown before dinner today, the assistants were asking Stale Bread a lot of questions about English.

"How do you say '*Gomen nasai*' in English?"

"I...beg...your...pardon," said Stale Bread trying to impress them.

"That's too hard. Is there a simpler way?"

"Very...sorry," he said, trying even harder to impress them.

"How about...'*Doozo odaiji ni*'?" asked another assistant.

"Please...tay-kyare...of...yourself," pronouncing "take care" as "tay-kyare."

He managed to sound even more pompous.

For some reason, the assistants heeded every word. Stale Bread's

English bothered Crazy Legs more than me. He whispered a song in his usual confident Dodoitsu,

> A doctor or Cabinet minister, someday he'll be.
> But now he's a great student with no money.

He was eager to rein in Stale Bread.

I'm feeling good. I was weighed today and had gained a little over three pounds. I am in great shape.

September 16

6

HYGIENE

1

I've been writing about the women for some time and have neglected reporting about my senior roommates. Today, I have news about the students of the Sakura Room. Today, we had a squabble in the Sakura Room. Crazy Legs fearlessly challenged Stale Bread. The clash was over dried plums.

It's a rather complicated tale. Crazy Legs had stored dried plums in a small Seto tea bowl. When it was time to eat, he took it from the lower shelf of his bed and poked at the dried plums. Unfortunately, mold had started to grow on them. Crazy Legs thought the container was bad. The lid of the bowl did not fit well and allowed bacteria to enter, and this led to mold. He was certain. Crazy Legs is the kind of person who likes hygiene. He's quite interested in it. Even before this incident, Crazy Legs had been reflecting on what would make a good container. During breakfast yesterday, from the corner of his eye, Crazy Legs spied an empty pickled scallion jar that Stale Bread carried to each meal and thought it would be suitable. It had a wide mouth and could be tightly shut. Bacteria would be unable to infiltrate that jar. And since it was empty, Stale Bread should have no problem lending it to him. Although the idea of thanking Stale Bread irked him, that pickled scallion jar was required to ward off bacteria. Hygiene must be respected. So thought Crazy Legs. After he finished his meal, Crazy Legs apprehensively presented his offer to Stale Bread to borrow the empty jar.

Stale Bread looked Crazy Legs in the face and asked, "What are you going to do with it?"

The way he asked threw Crazy Legs. A dark cloud had hovered between those two for some time. Crazy Legs had been appointed the ladies' man of The Health Dojo. As the upstart Stale Bread's rating as the ladies' man skyrocketed, Crazy Legs' profile dropped, and he was ticked off.

"What? Sugawa-san, you shouldn't speak like that?" said Crazy Legs coldly.

"Why can't I?" replied a stern Stale Bread. He is a rigid, pretentious man.

"Don't you understand?" said Crazy Legs who was losing ground and forced a smile, "It's not like I'm trying to borrow a pig's tail from you. Snapping at me puts me in an awkward position." Things were getting strange.

"I didn't say anything about a pig's tail."

"I don't understand you," said Crazy Legs, now a little bitter, "Even if you didn't say anything about a pig's tail, you knew exactly what I meant. Don't be a fool. College student, plasterer, aren't we both citizens of the same Japan? How dare you treat me like a pig's tail? If I'm a pig's tail, you're a lizard's tail. There is universal love. I don't have much education, but I do have respect for hygiene. People who are ignorant of hygiene are no different than animals."

What the hell was that? An utterly incomprehensible quarrel had erupted.

2

Stale Bread wasn't bothered in the least. He lay face up on his bed with his hands clasped behind his head. He looked like a man with pluck. Crazy Legs sat cross-legged on his bed, rocking. His sleeves were rolled up. He anxiously banged his knees with his fists.

"Hey, are you listening? Mr. Student. At least, no one will probably employ judo. Occasionally in college, you're afraid that there'll be some student who knows it. You'd apologize. I'll tell you straight. If this Dojo is not a judo dojo, it's definitely not a training dojo for ladies' men. Director Kiyomori said in a recent lecture, 'You are the players. The players who will show all of Japan evidence of a full recovery from tuberculosis.' He spoke of the fervent desire to take care of oneself. When I heard that, I cried. Unless a man sees justice, he loses courage. Courage demands both great courage and small courage. So for humanity, the three critical elements are wisdom, virtue, and valor. Being popular with women is not the problem at all."

Chaos reigned. Then, Crazy Legs' face paled and in a raised voice said, "So, because of that, I naturally came to the idea that hygiene is very important. I think that hygiene and being careful with fire are always important. One should never compare a person to a pig's tail."

"Stop it. Stop it now," intervened Echigo Lion. Until that moment, Echigo Lion had been lying quietly on his bed. He abruptly sat up and got off his bed. He slapped Crazy Legs' shoulder from behind and ordered him to stop.

Crazy Legs spun around toward Echigo Lion and hugged him. A sobbing Crazy Legs pressed his face into Echigo Lion's chest. Five or six puzzled students from the other rooms who were hanging out in the hall came to see what was happening.

"Get lost," bellowed Echigo Lion to the students in the hall. Everything had been great until then, but rapidly went downhill.

"It's not a fight! It's just... it's just...," he growled glaring at me.

"It's a play," I feebly offered.

"It's just...," then with renewed spirit, Echigo shouted, "It's the action from a play."

I don't know what "the action from a play" means, but your reputation may well be tarnished by repeating something straight from a youngster like me. I think that that unfamiliar phrase of "the action from a play" was devised on the spot and shouted out. It might be hard for an adult to live under these circumstances.

Crazy Legs resembled a lion cub nuzzled against his mother's breast. While sobbing and his face quivering, he began his appeal in a discouraged slur.

3

"I've never been so humiliated in my life. My upbringing was pretty bad. My father beat me. He pretty much treated me like a pig's tail and seethed with anger. I thought about a reasonable way to address you and said only the best thing. I thought that you just choose the best thing to say. Actually, my intent is to only say the best thing. In spite of that, you lie on the bed, pretending not to understand. Who acts like that! It's so annoying, you show no remorse. Who acts like that! A person says the best thing, but in return gets that attitude. Society becomes savage. A person says the best thing..."

He repeated the same thing over and over.

Echigo gently put Crazy Legs in bed. Crazy Legs lay down with his back to Stale Bread and covered his face with both hands. He was soon sobbing uncontrollably. Finally, he quieted down and seemed to have fallen asleep. He remained in that position even at 8 am, the time for the bending and stretching exercises.

It was truly a peculiar squabble. But around lunchtime, the old Crazy Legs had returned. Stale Bread brought over the empty washed pickled scallion jar and offered it to Crazy Legs. When he held it out sincerely and apologized, Crazy Legs gently took it with a slight bow. After lunch was over, he took the dried plums one by one from the Seto tea bowl and happily moved them to the pickled scallion jar. If everyone were a little like Crazy Legs, this world would definitely be a better place.

That's all I have to say about the fight. I have one more brief report.

This afternoon, Take-san did my rubdown. I told Take-san a little about you.

"There's someone who really likes you, Take-san."

Take-san said almost nothing during the rubdown. She just smiled coolly without saying a word.

"He said that Take-san is ten times better than Mabo."

"Who?" said Madame Mute softly. The person who praised her over Mabo was trusted. Women...so, so shallow.

"Are you happy?"

"I don't like it," said Take-san and continued with the rough rubdown. She was frowning and seemed to be in a bad mood.

"Are you mad? That person is really a nice guy. He's a poet."

"That's horrible. Skylark, you've been bad recently." She wiped the sweat from her forehead with the back of her left hand.

"Really? Tell me more."

Take-san said nothing. She continued the rubdown in silence. When the rubdown ended, she stood up and smoothed back her hair, and giggling said, "Very sorry."

She wanted to apologize. Take-san is not so bad. How about visiting the Dojo if you have the time? I want you to meet Take-san, whom you're so fond of. Just joking...sorry. It gets cooler everyday. Hygiene and being careful with fire are constants around here. We should study together.

September 22

7

COSMOS

1

I read your prompt reply with delight. Since you started college and are busy studying, you probably have a hard time writing long letters. From now on, you don't have to write such long detailed replies. I worry about interfering with your studies.

You scolded me about the inexcusable things I said to Take-san. I'm sorry. However, I cannot agree with your words of "I haven't been able to visit you yet." You are too timid. I'm trying not to be too much of a stickler, but if you can't greet Take-san, you can't be said to be a New Man. Sex appeal is thrown away. Don't the words "No evil thoughts" appear in the *Three Hundred Songs*? We should adopt an attitude of naiveté in all its glory.

A while ago, I said to my roommate Echigo Lion, "A friend of mine is studying poetry," Echigo promptly replied with disdain, "Poets are pretentious."

A little offended, I replied, "But haven't poets rejuvenated language for ages?" Grinning, Echigo Lion simply answered, "Well. If there is no new invention for today, it is bad." The things Echigo says are hard to dismiss.

Since you're a smart guy, I think you already know this, but, no matter what, you should continue studying poetry and show your true self as a New Man. I sounded a little cocky trying to mimic my elders. As for Take-san, I'm only saying not to worry about her. Gather your courage and come visit the Dojo to see Take-san with your own eyes. When you see the real thing, your illusions will evaporate. Anyhow, she's already a sea bream. You were devoted to Take-san. Although I emphasized Mabo's cuteness in my letter, you wrote, "A woman like Mabo resembles a washed-up movie actress." You understood nothing and only felt sorry for Take-san. I'll write soon about Take-san. You'll become fevered and have trouble sleeping.

Today, I will introduce Crazy Legs' haiku. Next Sunday's tranquility broadcast will present writings by the students. Confident students of tanka, haiku, and other poetry have until tomorrow evening to submit their works to the office. As a player on our Sakura Room team, Crazy Legs submitted a special haiku. I heard that he wrote for two or three days before the deadline. Sitting erect on his bed, his neck cocked, he solemnly composed his verse. This morning, he finally finished. He had written just ten verses on a writing pad and showed them to us, his roommates. First, he showed them to Stale Bread.

He smirked and said, "I don't understand this," and quickly handed the paper back.

Next, he asked Echigo Lion for his opinion. Echigo Lion hunched over and scrutinized the paper.

"Inexcusable," he said.

The criticism of "inexcusable" rather than saying "it's a little clumsy" or something else seemed cruel.

2

Crazy Legs paled and asked, "Is it bad?"

"Ask the professor over there," said Echigo and jerked his chin towards me.

Crazy Legs came over carrying his writing pad. Being uncultivated, I don't have a clue about the subtleties of haiku. Maybe, I should have replied promptly like Stale Bread, but I wanted to console poor Crazy Legs. Despite the problem of my lack of understanding, I read those ten verses.

They didn't seem that bad. The verses were mediocre or commonplace, but I probably would have struggled to write them.

Like the confused blooming of a chrysanthemum in a girl's mind

I thought that verse was a bit odd, but not horrible nor inept enough to make you angry. However, I was startled by the last verse. I understood Echigo Lion's anger.

This dewdrop world --
Is a dewdrop world,
And yet, and yet.

It was someone else's verse. Frankly, I didn't want to embarrass Crazy Legs, but this was unacceptable.

"All of them are pretty good, I think, but if you changed this last verse with another, it would probably be better. But that's the opinion of a mere novice."

"Yes...I see," said Crazy Legs pouting his lips a little dissatisfied. "I thought this was the best one."

It should be good. Even a haiku amateur like me recognized that famous poem.

"A good thing is good without a doubt."

I was a bit confused.

"I don't think you get it?" said Crazy Legs, "I think my sincerity towards today's Japan is woven into this poem. Can't you see that?" he said to me with a trace of contempt.

"What kind of sincerity?" I replied, no longer laughing.

"I don't think you understand?" Crazy Legs said that I was also a fool and frowned. He continued, "What do you think about Japan's fate now? It's an ephemeral world, a dewdrop world, right? This dewdrop world is a dewdrop world. Yet, doesn't the search for light continue? Doesn't it convey the meaning to never be pessimistic for any reason? This is my sincere devotion to Japan. Do you understand?"

I was astonished. This poem was by the haiku master Issa whose child had died, and he had resigned himself to the transience of the world. Isn't the intent of the poem to relay feelings of sadness and resignation? Well, that's terrible, isn't it? He twisted the meaning. This may be Echigo's so-called new invention of today, but it's pretty bad. Although I sympathize with Crazy Legs' sincerity, it stinks to steal a poem from an ancient master and stick on your own interpretation to amuse yourself. And if this poem were submitted to the office as Crazy Legs' work, the reputation of the Sakura Room would be affected. So I gathered my courage and said as much.

3

"Well, a poem by an ancient closely resembles this one. It may not be theft, but to prevent any misunderstanding, you should replace it with another."

"There's a poem like this one?"

Crazy Legs opened his eyes wide and stared at me. His eyes were so stunning I wanted to sigh. I thought that a self-satisfied poet of haiku might possess the strange mentality being unaware of theft. I reconsidered the situation. In fact, innocent criminals do exist. He is guileless.

"That one has become useless. This happens from time to time in haiku and is bothersome. There are just seventeen syllables. There are bound to be similar poems."

Crazy Legs seems to be a habitual offender.

"Yes, so I'll leave it out," he said with his pencil stuck behind his ear. He simply drew a line through the dewdrop world poem.

"How about this instead?"

He quickly wrote something at the small desk beside my bed and showed it to me.

The cosmos and the shadows dance, heaven perhaps.

"That's good," I said relieved. It may be poor, but I was relieved since it wasn't stolen. I was a bit too relieved and needlessly added, "So next, why don't you revise Cosmos?"

"Shadows of the cosmos dance, heaven perhaps.... Of course, the scene is more vivid. That's great," he said and slapped my back, "I can't fool you."

I blushed.

"You mustn't flatter me," I said still unable to relax, "I guess Cosmos is pretty good. I don't know a thing about haiku. But I feel like Cosmos is easy for us to understand."

My inner voice was shouting, "Is either one any good?"

But, Crazy Legs seemed to respect me. When he asked me to discuss haiku with him, I managed to keep a straight face confronted with all this flattery. With a triumphant feeling, he walked toward me, as he usually does, on his toes with that musical tapping walk and his butt swaying lightly. I watched him hoist himself onto my bed and felt out of my league. In reality, I find haiku discussions even more of a problem than those Monkukiri-style Dodoitsu poems. I couldn't settle down and was upset. Without thinking, I grumbled to Echigo, "This has gotten ridiculous."

The New Man was defeated by Crazy Legs' haiku.

Echigo Lion nodded in agreement.

But that's not the whole story. An even more surprising fact emerged.

This morning for the 8 am rubdown, it was Mabo's turn to give Crazy Legs a rubdown. What I heard Crazy Legs quietly say to her was amazing.

"Listen Mabo...your poem...that Cosmos poem...was pretty bad. Yeah...Cosmos...is awful."

What a surprise. Mabo wrote that poem.

4

That said, that strange poem seemed to have just a touch of a woman's sensibilities, as did the odd verse of "Like the confused blooming of a chrysanthemum in a girl's mind." Was that a poem written by Mabo or some other assistant? All ten of those haiku were suspect. The fact is, they are terrible people. I'm really disgusted about this. It's not an exaggeration to say that the dewdrop world poem and the cosmos poem affect the reputation of the Sakura Room. I was on edge about how to handle Crazy Legs' personality problem. But as I listened to the conversation between Crazy Legs and Mabo, I regained my peace of mind and began to feel much better.

"The cosmos poem. Which one was that? I've completely forgotten it," said Mabo unconcerned.

"Oh yeah...that was mine, wasn't it?" she asked indifferently.

"Wasn't that one Heatstroke's poem? When did you exchange haiku with Heatstroke? You did it secretly. Oh!"

"Looking at it, is it Heatstroke's poem?" she wondered. She seemed to be at a loss for the right words. Should she be candid or delicate?

"It's too good to be a poem by Heatstroke. Oh no! It was stolen."

The conclusion we had already reached. It could be nothing else with that flawless composition.

"This time, I'm going to submit this poem."

"For the tranquility broadcast? I'll submit mine with yours. When? Should I tell you? The one about the confused blooming in a girl's mind."

Just as I expected. But a nonchalant Crazy Legs said, "I'll submit that one."

"Oh. You're so conscientious."

I smiled.

To me, this was the so-called "Today's New Man." To these people, the author's name could be anyone. They work together to create. If they can enjoy it together one day, that's good. Isn't that the origin of the relationship between art and the masses? Liszt is second-rate only to Beethoven. This is what so-called "men of the world" argue about. The masses are left out of those arguments. Don't they carefully listen to and enjoy selections quickly made based on personal preference? The creators are not embraced by those people. Whether written by Issa, by Crazy Legs, or by Mabo, that poem is not interesting, it's bland. The compulsory study of art is not done for social etiquette or to elevate one's interests. Only a work that fills one's heart is remembered in one's own style. That's the only way. I felt like I would soon teach again about the relationship between art and the masses.

Today's letter was unusually cerebral, but I think that this anecdote about Crazy Legs is useful as a new invention in your poetry practice. I didn't tear up this letter, but sent it to you.

I am flowing water.
I flow brushing over every shore.
I love everyone.

Pretentious?

September 26

8

MY LITTLE SISTER

1

I'm always writing clumsy letters like this to you and sometimes am suddenly overcome with unsettling thoughts. I already decided three times not to write silly letters. But today I saw a truly great letter by someone and am in complete admiration of the absence of limits to greatness. Because a letter so ridiculous has been written in the world, I'm a little relieved that the letters I have sent you were mere misdemeanors. You know, many things happen in the world. That person composing a letter that makes you so mad that you suspect God or the Devil. Anyway, it's terrible.

So today, I will try to write one such great letter.

This morning was the Big Fall Clean-Up at the Dojo. The clean-up was nearly finished in the morning, so the afternoon routine turned into a rest period. Two barbers came from the barbershop, and it became haircut day for the students. Around 5 pm, my haircut was finished. While I was in the washroom washing my shaved head, someone came and stood beside me.

"Skylark, ya doin' it?"

It was Mabo.

"I'm doin' it. I'm doin' it," I pleasantly replied while lathering up my head with soap. Recently, this customary exchange has become irritating, annoying, and unbearable.

"Keep it up."

"Hey! Is my towel around here?" I didn't respond to the call of "Keep it up." With my eyes shut, I reached out both hands to Mabo.

She gently placed what felt like paper on my right hand. When I partly opened one eye, I saw a letter.

"What...is this?" I asked with a scowl.

An amused Mabo stared at me and said, "Skylark's meanness. Why didn't you say 'I got it'? A person who is told 'Keep it up' and can't respond with 'I got it' will get sicker."

I was disgusted. I was getting angrier, "Not here. I'm washing my hair. What is this? A letter?"

"It's from Horsetail. Is that a poem at the end? What does it mean?"

I squinted my eyes trying to keep the soap out and read the poem at the end of the letter.

> So many days without seeing you.
> Will it be soon? Are you hindered?
> I worry, my love.

I thought Horsetail was sophisticated.

"I don't get it. This is definitely a poem from the *Man'yoshu*. Horsetail did not write this poem." I didn't burn it up, but I did throw water on it.

"What does it mean?" she asked softly, leaning uncomfortably close to me.

"You're a pain! I'm washing my hair. I'll tell you later. Could you please put that letter down, and go get my towel? I think it's in my room. If it's not on my bed, it's in the drawer at the head of my bed."

"Meany!" Mabo snatched the letter from my hand and trotted off to my room.

2

Take-san's pet saying is "That's horrible," Mabo favors "Meany." I used to dread them saying these things, but I've grown accustomed to them, and they no longer bother me. While Mabo was gone, I had to think about what would be a good interpretation in the poem above of *ikani yokekuya* [Will it be soon? Are you hindered?] That phrase was troubling, I used the pretext of the towel to avoid having to answer immediately. I had to mull over how to interpret *ikani yokekuya*. When I washed off the soap, Mabo had to go get a towel. Soon she returned and solemnly handed over the towel without a word.

I was surprised and immediately felt guilty. Had I annoyed her or been inconsiderate? Recently, I had gotten used to life at the Dojo. The tension I first felt when I came here was gone. Even when I speak to Mabo and the others, I can no longer remember the agitation I felt before and have become desensitized. Naturally, the assistants are supposed to help the students, and may also think about special kindness and good ways to accomplish that. My brusque command to go and get my towel may have angered Mabo.

The other day, Take-san said, "Skylark can't do much these days." In fact, there are some things I haven't been able to do recently. During the Big Clean-Up this morning, all of the students went out to the garden in front of the annex for a while to escape the dust. I was grateful because it's been a long time since I've stood on the earth. Sometimes, I sneak down to the tennis courts out back. But this was the first time since I arrived that I had the proper permission to go out.

I stroked the trunk of a pine tree. The tree trunk was alive and warm like blood was coursing through it. I crouched down, surprised by the strong smell of grass at my feet, and scooped up some dirt in both hands. I was impressed by the weight of the dampness. To say nature lives is obvious, but a stronger feeling of realism comes with natural scents. But that wonder vanished in about ten minutes. Then I felt nothing. Numbness set in, and indifference returned. I became aware of that. Whether it was the habituation or the versatility of people, but I was disgusted with my helplessness. At that time, I thought long and hard about wanting to maintain that first new shudder about anything. Maybe, I had begun to slowly warm up to life at the Dojo, but in a flash, I'm mad at Mabo. Even Mabo has pride. It may be the small pride of a blooming violet, but that pathetic pride must be treasured. I ignored Mabo's friendship. Letting me see the private letter from Horsetail or Mabo's greater kindness to me than to Horsetail may be heartfelt actions that are wasted on me. No, even if I don't think with too much conceit, I have betrayed Mabo's trust. Saying that I don't like Mabo as much as before is my selfishness. Even I'm familiar with human kindness. I even forgot about the gift of the cigarette case. I'm no good. In fact, I'm horrible.

From now on, when "Keep it up," is called out, inspired by that kindness, I will shout out, "I got it!"

3

I must not delay in correcting my mistakes. The New Man quickly starts anew. When I left the washroom and went back to my room, I bumped into Mabo in front of the charcoal storeroom.

"Do you have the letter?" I immediately asked.

She had a vacant look, as if she were gazing off into the distance, and shook her head no.

Then I asked, "Is it in the drawer of my bed?" I thought that maybe she tossed the paper in the drawer when she went to get the towel earlier. She replied by only shaking her head. Women are awful because of things like this. They seem like cats that have been borrowed from some queer place. "Well, I'll do it my way," I thought, but I have a duty to value Mabo's pathetic pride in me.

I tried to cajole her, "Sorry about before. The meaning of that poem..."

"Forget about it," she said curtly and quickly left. She sounded a bit snide. I felt like I had been stabbed. Women are awful. I returned to my room and flopped down on my bed. My mind screamed, "That's it. I'm through."

However, at dinner that evening, Mabo brought my tray. Aloof, she placed the tray on the small desk at my bedside. On the way back, she went over to Stale Bread and told some silly joke like some kind of nut. She started to laugh boisterously and slapped Stale Bread's back. Stale Bread yelled, "Hey!" and tried to grab Mabo's hand.

"Eek," she shouted and escaped to me. She bent down bringing her lips to my ear and very quickly said, "Look at this and tell me what it means later," as she handed me a small folded letter and at the same time turned toward Stale Bread.

"Yo! Hey, Stale Bread, confess," she shouted, "Who was singing *Oedo Nihonbashi* at the tennis court?"

"I don't know. I don't know," said Stale Bread. He blushed as he tried hard to deny it.

"If it was *Oedo Nihonbashi*, I know," mumbled Crazy Legs, and he started to eat.

"Take care, everyone," said Mabo giggling as she bowed slightly and left the room. I had no idea what was going on. I felt like Mabo was making fun of me and was a little distressed. The letter remained in my hand. I didn't want to read someone else's letter. But I had to skim the letter to show appreciation for Mabo's small pride in me. Although I thought this had become a problem, I secretly read it after dinner. Well, the letter was magnificent. Maybe it's a love note, I have no idea. It's a complete surprise that the sensible, amiable, and mature Nishiwaki Horsetail wrote this ridiculous, absurd letter. A grown-up would probably hide this sweet silly side. Maybe I'll copy parts of this letter so you can see for yourself. I only read the end of the letter in the washroom. She passed me a total of three pages. I'll copy this great letter in its entirety below for you.

4

The letter begins with "The earth of past memories, the forests of the Dojo, I lean against the window sill and gaze as the waves break and retreat while in my mind I silently trace the affairs that should tell of a new page of life. Silently breaking and retreating waves...but the white waves roared. And the salty winds raged." Does that even mean anything? Of course, Mabo is baffled by this. This writing is harder to understand than the *Man'yoshu*.

Horsetail left the Dojo and went to a hospital in Hokkaido, his home. This hospital seems to be on the coast. That's about all I can understand, but what does the rest mean? I have no idea. It's unusual writing. I'll copy a little more for you. The text meanders and becomes more incomprehensible.

"When the evening moon sinks into the waves, when darkness blankets all, the light of the stars in the sky guide my soul to you, the world changes and tumbles. I will strive to live a proper life! I am a man! I am a man! I am a man!! I will carry on as a man. From now on, I would like to call you my little sister. Should I speak now of the natural gifts given to me? What should I say? I should speak of a lover full of passionate love."

I have no idea what that means. Then, the text gets even weirder, a surging wave of weirdness.

"To Masako,

"...That is neither a person nor an object, but is knowledge, the source of work. A lovable person from morning to night is science and the beauty of nature. Both together in one body should love me from the heart, and I too will love madly. I will gain a little sister and a lover, how happy I would be. My little sister! Mine!! I think you will understand from your heart this feeling, this heart's desire of mine, your big brother. I think that you're my little sister. I want you to send news about yourself. Do you understand? My little sister!!

"I'm sorry about this letter becoming so serious. I also apologize for calling the woman who has helped me, my little sister. Please try to understand. When you become a woman, it's a time to think about men and women and many other things, but be bold and don't think too deeply. I too will break from the mundane world. Today is a fine day, but the winds are strong. Nature is grand! I am drenched with tears and am not amused! I think you will understand. I carefully read your letter over and over today. Thank you. Stay strong, darling Masako!! My final words as a big brother, my dear little sister.

"So many days without seeing you. Will it be soon? Are you hindered? I'm worried, my love.

"From your big brother, Kazuo"

That's it. From your big brother Kazuo, what is that? It's weird writing "your big brother" with his name. I definitely miss the point of that verse from the *Man'yoshu* at the end. This is dreadful. I tried to copy it, but I can't write that stuff. You could say this is unprecedented. However, Nishiwaki Kazuo is in no way a lunatic. He's a kind, popular guy. A nice guy like that writing this kind of incoherent letter is one of the mysteries of this world. It's not outrageous for Mabo to say, "Tell me what it means." The recipient of this kind of letter is in a quandary. It must be distressing. Call it a literary gem or a magical verse, but copying this grand missive has worn out my wrist and turned my writing into scribbles. Bye for now. I'll write again soon.

October 5

9

THE TEST

1

The day before yesterday, I was overwhelmed by Horsetail's literary gem. My pen trembled so much I could no longer write. I apologize for that half-finished letter. After dinner that evening, when I read that letter, I was stunned. I saw Mabo peeking in through the window on the hall and asking with her eyes, "Have you read it?" I nodded yes. Mabo answered with a solemn nod. She seemed to be concerned about that letter. Nishiwaki was a criminal, I felt a strange indignation. Then I found Mabo unbearably sweet. I confess that since then I have found a renewed charm in Mabo. I had not become an insensitive man. Before I knew it, I had changed. I hate fall. Fall is a sad time. Stop laughing! This is serious.

Now, I'll tell you everything. The morning after the Big Clean-Up, Mabo suddenly appeared in the doorway carrying a metal basin under her arm for the 8 am rubdown. She came straight over to me looking like she was trying to keep from laughing. I didn't expect Mabo to get my number again so soon, and "Oh good," slipped out. I was happy.

"Cut it out," said an aggravated Mabo and immediately started my rubdown.

"Take-san drew you this morning, but she had other business. I'm her substitute. Okay?" she explained matter-of-factly. I was a little dissatisfied with this explanation, but said nothing. Mabo was also silent. The atmosphere became stifling. When I came to the Dojo, I was tense and felt awful when Mabo gave me a rubdown. Memories of that tension returned and so did my discomfort. Finally, the rubdown ended.

"Thanks," I said sounding sleepy.

"Give the letter back!" demanded Mabo in a whisper.

Lying on my back and frowning, I said, "It's in the drawer at the head of my bed." Clearly, I was irritated.

"Okay. Could you go to the washroom after lunch? Give it to me then." Without waiting for my reply, she got up and left.

She was strangely cold. When I show a little kindness, she immediately becomes unsociable. Well, if that's how it is, I'll have to think about this. I prepared a scathing criticism and waited for the noon rest time.

Take-san brought my lunch. A small bamboo doll was placed in a corner of the tray. I looked up at Take-san perplexed. Take-san frowned and furiously shook her head like she was saying tell no one. I nodded looking miserable. I don't get it, any of it.

2

"This morning, I went to town on urgent business for the Dojo," said Take-san in her usual voice.

"Is this a souvenir for me?" I asked, "Why?" sounding disappointed and uninterested.

"Isn't she cute? It's a Fuji Musume doll. A treasure," she said like a mature older sister and left.

I was stunned. Not even a little happier. Yesterday, the point was to reconsider when to be inspired by a person's kindness. What am I? I'm not grateful for Take-san's kindness to me. After all this time, I can't deny that I still feel like I haven't changed since coming to the Dojo.

Take-san is the supervisor of the assistants and a great person whom everyone at the Dojo relies on, and she must be dependable. Mabo is different. Take-san buys me this drab doll. Is Fuji Musume cute? Nope.

While eating, I never took my eyes off that small 2½-inch bamboo doll, known as Fuji Musume, in the corner of the tray. And the longer I looked at it, the more grotesque it became. What a lousy hobby. I'm sure this dusty shopworn doll came from the store at the station. Good-natured people are always poor shoppers. Take-san seems to be one of them. The delinquent Mabo is a practical shopper. Oh well. I am clueless about bamboo work. It even crossed my mind to give it back. Yesterday, I was primed with a commendable readiness to sympathize with the pathetic pride of the violet. Feeling dejected, I put away the souvenir in my bed drawer. Enough about Take-san, I'll stop here so you don't become fevered.

After lunch, I went to the washroom as instructed by Mabo. She was standing by the farthest wall with her back to me, chuckling. I immediately felt uncomfortable.

"You should do this every once in a while," I said, even surprising myself.

"Wh...Why?" she said looking up at me wide-eyed and trying to smile. I was spellbound.

"The students come here sometimes," I started to say while being dragged in, but I hesitated thinking about such indecent talk.

"Really? Then, let's get this over with," she said quietly and walked while bent forward as if bowing.

"I brought the letter," I said, taking it out.

"Thanks," she said as she took it without smiling.

"Skylark is bad after all."

"Why am I bad?" I meekly asked.

"You thought I was that kind of woman, Skylark?" she paled, looked into my eyes, and said, "Aren't you ashamed?"

"Yes," I simply admitted defeat. "I'm beaten."

Mabo laughed showing here sparkling gold tooth.

3

"I read that letter," I said with the intention of scolding her, but after getting that dumb Fuji Musume doll from Take-san, I was frustrated and felt guilty about Mabo. I didn't feel any better. When I went to the washroom feeling a little depressed, Mabo was so alluring, and I felt the most embarrassed and anxious as I ever had as a guy. Then I blurted out something unthinkable and immediately caused Mabo to reconsider. Now, it has all gone bad.

"I read it all. It was funny. Horsetail's a great guy. I really liked him," I said with insincere, foolish flattery.

"But, I didn't expect this letter," said Mabo slightly tilting her head, then she opened and stared at the letter.

"Yeah, I thought it was a little unexpected, too," I said clumsily and abruptly.

"It was totally unexpected." It suddenly seemed serious to Mabo.

"You seemed to have sent him a letter," I needlessly added and felt a chill.

"I did send him one," she said nonchalantly. I suddenly lost interest.

"So you seduced him. You look like a bad girl. It's called stupid. A fool, a tart, a strumpet, or a backstreet lover. Shameful," I said abusively. Far from being mad, Mabo laughed raucously.

"Listen to me. Horsetail is married. This is nothing to laugh at," I said.

"That's why I sent his wife a thank-you note. When Horsetail left the Dojo, I went with him to the station in town. His wife sent me two pairs of white *tabi* socks, so I sent her a thank-you note."

"That was it?"

"That's it."

"What?" my mood changed, "That was it?"

"Yup. Sending me that kind of letter was awful. It was agony."

"It's not good to agonize over anything. You really like Horsetail, don't you?"

"I like him."

"What?" Again I lost interest and said, "What a fool. How

stupid. Liking a married man is useless. They're a happily married couple."

"But would it be hopeless if I liked Skylark?"

"What are you saying? We're not talking about that," I said, I was aggravated, "You're not serious. I don't think you like me at all."

"Stupid dope. Skylark, you don't know anything. Skylark, doesn't know squat," she said as she turned around and burst into tears. Then she squirmed and shouted, "Go! Get out of here!"

4

I didn't know what to do. While pouting and wandering slowly around the washroom, I wanted to cry, too.

"Mabo," I called, my voice quivering, "Do you like Horsetail that much? I like Horsetail. He's a kind, good man. It's okay if you like him. Cry! Cry it all out. I'll cry with you."

Why did I say something that phony? Thinking about it now, it felt like a dream. I thought I was about to cry. But my eyes and head only burned, and not one tear came out. I opened my eyes wide and gazed out the window of the washroom at the gingko tree by the tennis court that had begun to turn yellow.

"Hurry!" said Mabo who was suddenly at my side, "Go back to your room. Make sure nobody sees you. That would be bad," she said in a tone so quiet and calm that it was scary.

"I don't care if anyone sees me. I'm not doing anything wrong," I said with my heart pounding a bit.

"Don't be a fool, Skylark," she said while standing next to me looking out the window of the washroom at the tennis court, and as if talking to herself said, "The Dojo really changed after Skylark came. He probably doesn't know that? Skylark's father is an important man. The director said so. They say he's a world famous scholar."

"Poor, but world renown," I said feeling very lonely. I hadn't seen my father in two months. As usual, I blew my nose so loud the shoji screen shook.

"You come from good stock. When Skylark came, the Dojo quickly brightened. Everybody felt different. Even Take-san said that they had never seen such a wonderful child. Take-san rarely praises anyone, but she was fascinated with Skylark. And not only Take-san, Goldfish, Onion, everyone it seems. Everyone had to be careful and not approach Skylark because we couldn't let someone start a disgusting rumor among the students that would cause trouble for Skylark."

I forced a smile. "What a stingy love," I thought.

"So, this keeping a respectful distance. I don't like it."

"What?...Oh that," said Mabo and gently tapping me on my back, then lightly resting her hand there, "I'm different. I don't like Skylark at all. So talk about the two of us alone wouldn't bother me. Don't misunderstand me. I..."

I moved away from Mabo and said, "By all means, write to Horsetail. I clearly say that, but I was disgusted by the crassness of Horsetail's letter."

"I know. I had you look at the letter because it was crass. If it had been a nice letter, nobody would have seen it. I don't think about Horsetail. I don't make fun of people like that," she said in the words and attitude of another person, blunt and vulgar, "I'm no good. You know that? You don't see it because you're a dope. Everyone says that I have a good relationship with you. Well? Is that okay?"

Giggling, she turned her face, jutted out her right shoulder, and pushed me hard.

5

"Stop, quit it," I said. I had nothing else to say at that time. It had gotten absurd.

"Am I bothering you? What are you gonna do? Are you ashamed? Last night, the moon was bright and I couldn't sleep. So I went out to the garden, then I opened the curtain at Skylark's bedside just a bit and peeked in. Did you know that? You were asleep and smiling under the moonlight. That sleeping face was lovely. Skylark, what are you gonna do?"

She pushed me against the wall. I looked so stupid.

"That's too much. Come on. I'm twenty. This is bad. Wait...someone's coming." I heard the sound of slippers coming to the washroom.

"No, that's not it," said Mabo as she walked away. She turned her face upward, pulled her hair up with both hands, and burst out laughing. She turned so red like her face had been splashed with hot water.

"It's lecture time. I gotta go. I'll be late. I hate being lax."

I ran out of the washroom, just as Mabo quietly said, "Don't get too friendly with Take-san." Her voice pierced my heart.

I hate the fall.

When I returned to my room, the lecture hadn't begun yet. Crazy Legs was lying on his bed singing a Dodoitsu poem as usual. I've heard that Dodoitsu poem many times. It was about how grass on the road rejuvenates in the morning dew even after being trodden on by people. Strangely, only that time, I didn't feel my usual embarrassment and quietly listened. I may have become weak.

The lecture soon began. The topic was the interactions between the Japanese and Chinese civilizations. A young professor named Okaki gave an easy-to-understand lecture with various examples from long ago mainly of medical exchanges. I found the examples convincing and reflecting the fact that Japan and China were and still are countries that have advanced by learning from each other. Still, today's secret bothered me. I was intent on quickly forgetting about Mabo and becoming a carefree model student again.

Mabo is impossible. If I thought she were a little smarter, she would be surprisingly stupid. I already described her unbelievable antics, but even I know they mean nothing. I have none of that stupid conceit. Mabo always thinks only of herself. Horsetail and I aren't the problem. She wants to be enchanted with her own beauty and misery. Although she feigns innocence, she probably won't let anyone defeat her. And because she's so greedy, she probably wants anything anyone else has. However, I can see through her schemes.

6

Mabo probably wanted to boast a little about showing me Horsetail's letter. But Mabo was sensitive to my ridiculing that letter. Her attitude changed and definitely resulted in the crying, pushing, and crazy talk. She resembles a queen with the pride of a violet and high opinion of herself. I have absolutely no sympathy. Everyone's probably making fun of us when they said that Mabo and I are close. How stupid. I've never given others a reason to make fun of Mabo. She alone is stirring up trouble. Mabo has zero discretion and is the product of a truly bad upbringing. As Echigo said, maybe her mother was lacking. As I tried to calm down, I got angrier. I don't think she is qualified to be an assistant at the Dojo. The Dojo is a sacred place. If Mabo behaves so boldly again, I'm resolved to appeal to her supervisor Take-san and have Mabo exiled from the Dojo.

If I were that resolved, I wouldn't be so bothered about the nightmare in the washroom.

That was a nightmare. The nightmare has no connection to life. I had a dream in which I beat you up, but didn't apologize the next day. I don't have the heart of a sentimental man of religion or a poet. The New Man despises complexity.

I didn't intend to make a big deal about dreams, but the day after the nightmare in the washroom, that is, before daybreak this morning, I had another dream. This was a good dream. You don't want to forget a good dream. I want it to hold some kind of connection to life. I really want to tell you, too. It was a dream about Take-san. Take-san is a good person. I truly thought so this morning. People like her are rare. I thought it was easy for you to be smitten with Take-san. You are only a poet with a sharp intellect. You have a sharp eye and are an admirable man. Since Take-san gives you a fever, I thought sleeping with her would be a problem. So my report about Take-san was guarded, that kind of worry was totally unnecessary. I understood that this morning.

No matter how much someone likes Take-san, she is not the type who would be depraved and sleep with that person. That made me like Take-san even more. I won't let you outdo me and I intend to trust Take-san even more. That said, Mabo is a dumb woman. She is the exact opposite of Take-san. As I've described her, she is like a good-for-nothing movie actress. Yesterday, Mabo came to the Sakura Room even though she hadn't drawn my number for the 8 pm rubdown. She gabbed with Stale Bread and Crazy Legs as if she had completely forgotten what had happened that day. Take-san gave me the rubdown in silence, but as usual, the rubdown reflected her adept technique. Sometimes she smiled at the stupid jokes of Mabo and the others. Mabo strutted over to our side and jokingly said, "Take-san, need some help?"

Take-san bowed slightly and said, "Thank you, but I'm almost finished."

7

I like Take-san who is calm and composed in these kinds of situations. When showing a clumsy friendliness to me, Take-san does not seem awkward. When Mabo spun around and returned to Stale Bread, I whispered to Take-san, "Mabo's a phony."

"She has a good heart," Take-san tersely replied.

At that time, I harbored the thought that Take-san was superior to Mabo. Take-san soon finished the rubdown, grabbed the metal basin, and went next door to the Swan Room to help. Then, the laughing Mabo came over to my bed and whispered, "Whaddya say to Take-san? Tell me. I want to know."

"I said you're a phony."

"Meany! Why would you say that?" Surprisingly, she didn't get mad.

"Hey, do you have it?" she asked forming the fingers of both hands into a square.

"The case?"

"Yeah. Where do you keep it?"

"In the drawer over there. I'll give it back."

"What?! No. You must keep it your whole life, although it may be an inconvenience," she solemnly said. Suddenly she shouted,

"Of course, Skylark's bed is the best spot to see the moon. Crazy Legs come here quickly! Look at the moon from here. You should recite *Meigetsu* or some other haiku. How about it?"

She's so boisterous.

That kind of incident that night was not particularly unusual and I easily fell asleep, but at daybreak, I suddenly awoke. My room was dimly lit by the light left on in the hall. I checked the clock beside my bed, it was a little before five and still dark outside. I saw someone from my window. I immediately recognized Mabo! Her face was white. She was definitely laughing, then disappeared in a flash. I leapt up and threw back the curtain to look, but there was no one. That felt weird. Maybe I was still half asleep. I really thought Mabo was a ridiculous person. Surprisingly, I'm also a romantic and with a wry smile I flopped back into bed, but I was a little worried. Moments later, I could hear the faint sound of water, like someone was washing something, coming from the distant washroom.

It's her! I thought. I don't know why, but I knew it was that laughing woman who had disappeared. It was definitely her over there. I couldn't stand it, so I quietly got up and crept out to the hall.

A lone blue bulb lit the washroom. I peeked in and saw Take-san wearing a white apron over a kimono with a splash pattern. She was crouched down scrubbing the washroom floor. A towel was wrapped around her head, and she resembled an *Oshima Anko*, a maiden of Oshima. She looked back and saw me, but continued washing the floor without saying a word. Her face seemed gaunt. All the residents of the Dojo were still fast asleep. Does Take-san always get up so early and start cleaning? I was speechless, but my heart was pounding when I saw the figure of Take-san cleaning. I confess that was the first time in my life I was tormented by a formidable lust. In the deep darkness just before daybreak, I squirmed at that extraordinary sign.

8

This washroom is my unlucky spot.

"Take-san...earlier...," I said gasping, my voice caught in my throat, "Were you in the garden?"

"No," she turned toward me, smiling a little and said, "What are you saying, sleepyhead? Oh, you're horrible. Are you barefoot?"

I hadn't noticed, but I was. In my excitement, I forgot to put on my sandals.

"A problem child. Wipe off your feet."

Take-san stood and rinsed out a cloth in the sink, then came over to me and wiped the soles of my right then my left foot. She not only took an interest in my feet, but in the depths of my heart. That strange, formidable lust vanished.

As Take-san washed my feet, my hands rested on her shoulders. "Take-san, will you keep on pampering me?" I said trying to mimic her Kansai accent.

"Oh, you're lonely," said Take-san without a hint of humor, like she was talking to herself. She took off her slippers and held them out to me, and said, "Here, take these. Hurry and do your business. Good night."

"Thanks," I said nonchalantly and put on the slippers, "I'm probably half asleep."

"Didn't you wake up because you had to use the bathroom?" said Take-san in a mature tone as she resumed washing the floor.

"Well, yes...but..."

I couldn't tell her something as foolish as I saw a woman's face outside my window. Maybe I saw some kind of phantom because my soul is impure. I felt ashamed and embarrassed thinking that I got here because I was excited by my dirty mind and ran out to the hallway barefoot. But there is also a person who wakes in the dead of night every night to silently and diligently clean.

Leaning against the wall, I gazed at Take-san's moving figure for a moment and keenly understood the gravity of life. I thought that health has this form. Thanks to Take-san, the ball of purity in my heart became more transparent.

You're an honest guy. An uncomplicated, upright guy. Up to now, I despised Take-san's goodness a little, but that was wrong. You have a keen eye. Mabo can't compare. Take-san's love can't corrupt a person. This is important. I intend to become a person with that kind of pure love. I'll soar higher day by day. The air is slowly getting colder.

A man's life is touch and go. The New Man always plays, nimbly slips through, and flies in dangerous places.

When I think like this, the fall isn't bad. A little autumn chill feels good.

A dream of Mabo is a nightmare and I want to forget it soon, but if a dream of Take-san is like this, I never want to wake up.

A lover? No.

October 7

10

STALE BREAD

1

Greetings,

The winds are fierce. It may be a windstorm. The American Occupation Army is probably surprised, too. It appears that four or five hundred people have come to E City, but none of them has been seen around here. The director also gave words of caution to not become needlessly frightened or a laughingstock, and for everyone at the Dojo to stay calm. Only one assistant, Goldfish, looked forlorn and was teased by everyone. Two or three days ago, Goldfish had to go to E City for business in the rain. She returned to the Dojo, went to bed with everyone, but then she cried in despair. Everyone asked What's wrong? What happened? While sobbing convulsively, Goldfish related the following incident.

Goldfish had finished her business in town and was waiting at the bus shelter for the bus back to the Dojo. During the downpour, an empty American truck that was approaching seemed to break down and stopped a little ahead of the bus shelter. Two boyish American soldiers jumped down from the cab and started to fix the truck while being pounded by the rain. They didn't seem to be making much progress. They fiddled with the engine in silence looking like drenched rats. Soon the bus came for Goldfish and the others, Goldfish ran out of the bus shelter to get on the bus. As if in a dream, she gave a pear from her parcel to each of these American youths and heard voices from behind her say, "Thank you." The bus departed right after she boarded. That was it. She returned to the Dojo and gradually calmed down, but she filled with an indescribable, unbearable anxiety. That night, she covered herself completely with a futon and began to sob. By the next morning, this news had quickly spread throughout the Dojo. The understanding people, the rude people, and the clueless people all had a big laugh. Goldfish didn't find the teasing funny, she just shook her head and remained anxious.

Around that time, my roommate Stale Bread had been glum. He seemed to be tormented and experiencing some unusual troubles.

Stale Bread is secretive, pretentious, remote, doesn't associate with us at all, and is very controlled. The night before last, we had a blackout a little after seven because of those winds. As a result, we didn't have the evening rubdown. And we couldn't hear the evening report because the blackout also shut off the loudspeaker. The students all turned in early. But the winds roared and no one could sleep. Crazy Legs softly sang. Echigo Lion pulled out a candle from a drawer of his bed, lit it, and placed it at his bedside. Sitting cross-legged on his bed, he diligently mended his slippers.

"These winds sure are strong," said Stale Bread coming over to us while snickering. It was truly a rare event for Stale Bread to go over to someone else's bed for amusement.

2

I thought that people, like moths drawn to light, may be drawn together on stormy nights like this to the dim light of a candle.

"Yes," I said sitting up to greet him, "The Occupation Army is probably surprised by this storm."

"No, no, that's not it," he said in a slightly jocular tone, oddly laughing and smiling, "The problem is the Occupation Army. Please read this," and handed a letter to me.

The letter was filled with English.

"I can't read English," I said blushing.

"You can read it. Guys your age have been learning English since high school. We've already forgotten it," he said laughing. He sat on the end of my bed, and in a whisper that only I could hear, he quickly said, "The truth is, I wrote this English. There are probably grammatical errors, and I'd like you to correct them. You'll see when you read it, but the people in this Dojo overrate me as a master of English. If American soldiers come to the Dojo, I may be called to interpret. I got worried thinking about it. Please understand." He laughed a little to hide his embarrassment.

"But isn't your English pretty good?" I said glancing at the letter.

"This is no joke. It's not good enough to interpret. I was a little too confident and bragged a bit too much to the assistants. Can't you see that if I'm asked to interpret and they see me flustered, who knows how much respect they'll lose for me. Nothing could be more pathetic. I've been so worried about this lately that I haven't been sleeping well at night. I beg you," he said, again laughing.

I read the English in the letter. There were words I didn't know sprinkled throughout, but the English seemed to mean this.

Dear Sir,

Don't get mad. Please forgive my rudeness. I am a pitiful man. I listen and speak English, and other things all like the child. They are too hard to me, but I have go to Canada. And besides I am sick with tuberculosis. You watch out! Dangerous! There is big chance of you get disease. But I have much trust in you. I see you are fine gentleman. I know you have sympathy for this pitiful man. My English talking is very bad, and I read and write only little. If you have kindness and patience, please write on paper here your business here today. Please be patient for one hour. In that time, I will shut myself in my room and study your writing, and will answer with my best ability.

I pray hard for your good health. Don't be mad at my poor, ugly writing.

3

Compared to Horsetail's mysterious incomprehensible letter, this one was as logical as could be expected. But I couldn't help not finding the letter hilarious. Stale Bread feared being recruited to interpret. Because of his usual sense of superiority, I can surmise from this English writing that he has toiled and suffered to devise various machinations in order to not wind up being embarrassed and to avoid betraying the expectations of the assistants in the rare event he were called into action.

"This looks like a pivotal diplomatic document. It's quite impressive," I said stifling laughter.

"This isn't a joke," said Stale Bread with a forced smile as he snatched the letter from me. "Are there any mistakes?"

"No, it's very easy to understand. This could probably be called fine prose."

"Fine prose for the lost, perhaps?" he quipped. Nevertheless, he didn't seem to feel bad about being praised and took on a look of rationality with a tinge of pride. He lamented with a small affected sigh, "Being an interpreter is a great responsibility and of great importance. So I thought about it and took the liberty of writing that letter. I had displayed my knowledge of English too much, so I may be drafted to interpret. I can't escape now and it has become a burden."

I was struck by the variety of worries that weigh on people.

Maybe it's the fault of the storm or the dim light, but that night in our room, the four of us gathered around the light of Echigo Lion's candle and, for the first time in a long time, conversed with each other.

For some reason, Crazy Legs whispered, "What on earth is a liberal person?"

"In France," said Stale Bread, who should have learned his lesson with English, to announce his knowledge of France. He pompously added with raised eyebrows, "Men called Libertines revered free thought and ran amok. That was in the 17th century, about 300 years ago. They primarily called for freedom of religion and ran riot."

"What? They ran riot?" asked Crazy Legs with a surprised look on his face.

"Yes, well...they seemed to have lived the lives of scoundrels. The big-nosed Cyrano made famous by the play was said to have been a libertine in those days. He opposed the authorities of the day and aided the weak. Most of the French poets of that time seemed to have been that way. They bear a few similarities to the *otokodate*, the Robin Hoods of the Edo period in Japan."

"So...it's..," Crazy Legs blurted, "So Banzuin Chobei, the street fighter against injustice, was a liberal."

4

But an unsmiling Stale Bread said, "That doesn't matter. A libertine in the 17th century in France was usually like that, but today's liberal is a little different. The samurai and otokodake Hanakawado Sukeroku and the heroic thief Nezumikozou Jirokichi may have been liberals."

"Oh, so that's what it means," said a delighted Crazy Legs.

Echigo Lion grinned while mending the tear in his slipper.

More seriously, Stale Bread said, "The original form of free thought is a rebellious spirit. It may be called destructive thought. These are not the thoughts that initially arose in the removal of oppression and shackles, but are the thoughts of fighting that arose in concert with reactions to oppression and shackles. Although there are many examples, one day a dove asked the gods, 'When I fly, the air becomes a barrier and I cannot move forward quickly. I would like you to make the air go away.' The gods listened to this wish. Then, however, no matter how hard the dove flapped, he could not fly. This dove has free thought. First, the air has resistance, and the dove can fly. Free thought with no target for struggle is like a dove flapping in a vacuum tube, and is unable to soar."

"Is there another name for that man?" asked Echigo Lion taking a break from mending his slipper.

"Ah," said Stale Bread scratching the back of his head, "Nothing was said with that meaning. This is Kant's example. I know nothing about the modern Japanese political world."

"But you must know a little. From now on, all young people will be given the right to vote and the right to run for office," said Echigo, calmly like the elder of the group.

"The content of free thought was entirely different in those days. The geniuses who pursued and fought for the truth were known as free thinkers. I think the originator of free thought was Christ. Is an amazing example of free thought not to worry and just to 'look at the flying bird, it neither sows nor reaps nor gathers'? I believe that Western thought is entirely based on, or elaborates on, or is familiar with, or is skeptical of the spirit of Christ, and as a result, the various views held by people, in the end, are tied together in the Bible. Even science is not unrelated to this. The foundations of science are all hypotheses in the worlds of physics and chemistry. They originate from a hypothesis that cannot be seen with the naked eye. All sciences are created from the belief in this hypothesis. The Japanese people should study the Bible before studying Western philosophy and science. I'm not a Christian, but without also studying the Bible, Japan only studied the surface of Western culture, and I believe that to be the true reason for the crushing defeat of Japan. In free thought, in anything, they can't even understand half of what there is to know without knowing the spirit of Christ."

5

Everyone was silent for a while. Even Crazy Legs appeared to be in deep meditation and silently shook his head.

"Examples abound of the substance of free thought changing from moment to moment," eloquently said Echigo Lion that night. He had the charm found in some kind of noble recluse.

In fact, many people are probably like that. Nowadays, I secretly believed that there may be people capable of vital work for the nation, if their bodies are healthy.

"Long ago in China, there was a lone freethinker who opposed the authorities of the day and in a rage hid deep in the mountains. There was no benefit for him at that time. He was unaware that that was his defeat. He possessed a celebrated sword. When the time came, he was confident that holding this celebrated sword, he would run through his political adversaries and then hide in the mountains. Ten years passed, and the world changed. When the time came, he descended from the mountains and taught others about his freethinking, but they were only trite opportunistic thoughts. Finally, he drew the celebrated sword to show the people his heart, but his talk was so sad and already stale. This means that over a long period of time, immutable political ideas are nothing more than delusions.

"Free thought in Japan since the Meiji period initially was opposition to the Shogunate, then the denunciation of clan favoritism, followed by attacks on the bureaucracy. At times like this, shouldn't a man of virtue recite the words of Confucius about sudden change? In China, a man of virtue is different from the trustworthy man who neither drinks nor smokes in Japan and seems to mean a genius in the Six Arts. He may also be called a genius man of ability. This, after all, is sudden change. A beautiful change is displayed. It differs from dishonorable betrayal.

"Christ also says to take a vow. He also said to think about tomorrow. In fact, isn't he the great master of freethinkers? The freethinker laments, 'foxes have dens, birds have nests, but the son of man has no place to lay his head.' One day of living in peace is not allowed. Conviction must be renewed each and every day. The military bureaucracy of yesterday in Japan was attacked; that is not free thought. That is opportunism. If a true freethinker, you must put things aside and cry out."

"What is it? What should you cry out?" Crazy Legs asked hastily.

"Don't you know?" said Echigo Lion sitting erect, "'Banzai! Long live the Emperor!' This cry was old until yesterday. Today, however, this is the newest free thought. The reason of ten years ago differs from the reason of today. That is not mysticism after all. It is the innate love of humanity. The true freethinkers of today should die based on this cry. America is said to be a free country. They will surely recognize this cry of freedom in Japan. If I weren't sick now, I would stand before the bridge at Niju-bashi [the main gate of the Imperial Palace] and shout, 'Banzai! Long live the Emperor!'"

Stale Bread took off his glasses. He was crying. On that stormy night, I came to love Stale Bread. He's a good man. This has nothing to do with the problem of Mabo and Take-san. That concludes the news from the Dojo entitled "The Light of the Storm." Bye.

October 14

11

LIPSTICK

1

Thanks for writing back. I'm glad you liked my letter the other day about the conversation on a stormy night. I gather that in your opinion Echigo Lion may be a great politician rarely seen these days or a renowned teacher, but I don't think so. On the contrary, this is the age of an anonymous public blurting out opinions. The leaders only lose their minds and run around in confusion. In this situation, it is clear that the public is being abandoned. A general election is approaching, but all we hear are weird speeches that result in the public increasingly making fun of the representatives.

Speaking of elections, an odd incident occurred at the Dojo today. A little after noon, the following flyer was issued by our neighbors in the Swan Room.

"The matters at hand are the inability to endure the hearty congratulations for giving women the right to vote and the unbearable sight of the assistants at the Dojo plastered with heavy make-up. The right to vote also cries. We've heard stories of the American Occupation Army Forces mistaking garish-looking women wearing lipstick for prostitutes, as they should well be. Not only does this disgrace the Dojo, but it brings shame to all Japanese women. Therefore, the nicknames of all assistants whose make-up is too conspicuous shall be entered onto a list."

Then they added, "Of the top six names, the make-up of Peahen is the most hideous, she looks like the Monkey King eating horsemeat. We have tried often to advise her, but to no avail. She should be banished from the Dojo."

For some time, the Swan Room next door has held men of principle. Stale Bread, who is popular among the assistants, and others couldn't stand living in the Swan Room and fled to the Sakura Room. Thanks to the charm of Echigo Lion, the Sakura Room is a cheerful, genial place. The flyer was awful. Crazy Legs called for dissent. A grinning Stale Bread backed Crazy Legs.

"Isn't this terrible?" asked Crazy Legs as he sought support from Echigo Lion, "I think humanity is universal love and no one should be banished. The natural love of humanity is not to be forgotten under any circumstances."

Echigo Lion nodded slightly and remained silent.

Invigorated by this, Crazy Legs said, "That's right, isn't it? Free thought does not mean this kind of selfishness. What do you think, young professor? Is my argument wrong?" to encourage my agreement.

Still laughing, I said, "Will those guys next door really try to banish people? They're showing everyone their true sentiments."

"No, no it doesn't," argued Crazy Legs, "To begin with, I believe a fatal contradiction lies between women's right to vote and lipstick. Those guys usually aren't popular with the ladies. Without a doubt, this is a plan for revenge."

2

Then, as usual, came the best comment.

"Real courage and physical courage co-exist in the world. Those guys have physical courage. I hate it when they call me Shaved Pubes. That has bugged me for a long time. I don't like the nickname Crazy Legs much, but I can't keep silent when called Shaved

Pubes." With unexpected indignation, he got off the bed, fixed his belt, and said, "I will hit back at this flyer. Free thought has been around since the Edo period. People have not forgotten wisdom, virtue, and valor. Fellows, leave it to me. I intend to strike back at this." His complexion was changing color.

"Wait, wait," said Echigo Lion while rubbing the tip of his nose. "You can't go. We must leave it to the professor."

"To... Skylark?" asked Crazy Legs, who seemed upset, "Pardon me, but isn't it too much to ask of Skylark? For a long time, I've had problems with those guys next door. It's not something that has just started. They say Shaved Pubes, then retreat into silence. This is a matter of freedom and shackles. A wise man adapts to freedom and shackles. Those guys have absolutely no understanding of the spirit of Christ. If the situation demanded, I could make a show of force. That would be hard for Skylark."

I got off my bed, slipped in front of Crazy Legs, and grabbed the flyer from him and said, "I'll be right back," as I left the room.

The Swan Room had been waiting impatiently for the reply from the Sakura Room. When I arrived, all eight students mobbed me.

I was met by scattered comments in good cheer.

"Well, an incisive proposal, right?"

"The pretty boys of the Sakura are probably weak."

"They won't betray us."

"A united front of all students will call on the director to banish Peahen. What a waste to give the right to vote to that Monkey King."

They all looked like innocent mischievous children.

"Can I do it?" I shouted above everyone.

There was a hushed silence for a short time, then pandemonium.

"Don't interfere. Don't interfere."

"Is Skylark the envoy of compromise?"

"The Sakura Room lacks grit. Now is a crucial time for Japan."

"It may have fallen to a fourth rate country. Doesn't it see a pretty face and slobber all over it?"

"What? You said let me do it. That's a surprise."

"Tonight, by bedtime," I yelled while standing on my toes. "I'll report back, if you don't like my plan, I'll follow your proposal."

Again, there was silence.

3

After a few moments, a thirty-year-old with frightening eyes called Rat Snake asked, "Do you oppose our plan?"

"I'm in full agreement. Your plan intrigues me. Let me do it. Please."

Everyone seemed to deflate a little.

"All right. Thank you. Let me borrow this flyer until tonight," I said and quickly exited the room. That was it. It wasn't hard. Later, I would ask Take-san.

When I returned to my room, a frustrated Crazy Legs said, "Skylark was a bad idea. I went down the hall and eavesdropped. Nothing will come of it. The spirit of Christ and the wisdom to change would have been a powerful punch. 'Freedom and shackles!' would have been good to say. Those guys don't understand reason, and logical expression is paramount. Why didn't you say that free thought is air and a dove?"

I only said, "Leave it to me until tonight," and lay down on my bed.

I was actually a little tired.

Lying down, Echigo said in a dignified voice, "Leave it to him. Leave it to him." Crazy Legs said no more and reluctantly went to bed.

I had no plan. However, I was optimistic about Take-san's help when I showed her the flyer. During the bending and stretching exercises at 2 pm, Take-san passed by our room and glanced at me. I instantly summoned her with a small gesture of my right hand. She gave a subtle nod and promptly entered the room.

"Do you need something?" she asked seriously.

While moving my legs, I whispered, "The pillow...the pillow."

Take-san saw the flyer on the pillow, picked it up, and scanned it. "Let me borrow this," she coolly said and slipped the flyer under her arm.

"It's never too late to change one's ways. The sooner the better."

Take-san with a knowing look, nodded, then walked over to the window at the head of my bed and gazed out at the view.

Moments later, she said in an unadorned tone out the window, "Gen-san, you've been hard at work." Beneath the window was Gen-san, the elderly handyman who had begun weeding two or three days earlier.

"Well, the *Obon* Festival has just passed," said Gen-san from below, "I've weeded once, but this has already grown back."

I was moved by the resonance in Take-san's voice when she said, "You've been hard at work." I also felt serene, unconcerned about the flyer. But more than that, I was struck by the dignity ringing through her kind voice. Her leisurely tone was that of the wife of a great landowner calling from the veranda to the guard of the inner garden. She seemed to have been very well raised. Echigo once said that Take-san's mother was undeniably a woman of high standing. By leaving it to Take-san, this heavy make-up incident would be skillfully resolved to my great relief.

4

My reward for that trust was fantastic, beyond my expectations.

During nature time at 4 pm, suddenly from the loudspeaker in the hall, we heard the voice of a staff member say, "Please remain...Please relax and listen where you are. The make-up of the assistants has been a problem for some time. Therefore, the assistants have voluntarily submitted a remedy for today only."

We heard shouts of joy from the Swan Room.

The special broadcast continued, "Between dinner and the 7:30 pm rubdown this evening, each assistant will wash off her make-up to not create awkward misunderstandings by the Americans, then appear before the students. Next, the assistant Makita-san has a word for the students. Please consider the pure heart of Makita-san."

Makita-san is usually called Peahen. Peahen quietly cleared her throat and said, "I myself..."

Next door, they burst out laughing. Even in our room, everyone was smiling.

"I myself..." she said in a small cute voice like the chirping of a cricket, "For the time and the place, I have been inconsiderate and ill mannered despite being the oldest. I wish to apologize. In the future, kindly guide me."

We heard, "Good. Good," from next door.

"How pitiful," said Crazy Legs quietly and looked at me out of the corner of his eye. I was pained.

Then the staff member said, "We close with this request from all of the assistants. They would like Makita-san's nickname to be changed immediately. This concludes today's special broadcast."

Another flyer swiftly came from the Swan Room.

"We are all completely satisfied and appreciate the efforts of Skylark. Peahen should be dubbed I'myself."

Crazy Legs immediately announced his opposition to this proposal for her nickname. The nickname I'myself would be too cruel.

"It's heartless. She spoke to the best of her ability. Didn't they say to consider her pure heart? It's like watching flying birds. Isn't there universal love for all things? To curse another is to curse yourself. I am absolutely opposed. Because without her face powder, Peahen's black skin will be visible. In that case, would it be okay to change her name to Crow?"

That would be both savage and cruel. It would also be pointless.

A chuckling Echigo said, "Well, Peahen is simple, drop the first syllable of Peahen to create Hen."

I wrote on the flyer that Hen is sensible and not very funny, but in the opinion of an elder, I'myself is too cruel and Hen is good enough, then I handed the flyer to Crazy Legs.

The Swan Room was flooded with nickname proposals from all the other rooms. In the end, I'myself may be chosen. For one, the slight throat clearing by Peahen at that time and her saying "I myself" were unforgettable. And all of the nicknames other than I'myself felt bland.

5

For the 7:30 pm rubdown, Goldfish, Mabo, Heatstroke, and Take-san each carried a basin to the Sakura Room. The composed Take-san came straight over to me. Goldfish and Mabo were counted among the people cautioned about make-up. Looking at them when they came to our room that night, their hairstyles seemed a little different, but they were still wearing make-up.

"Is Mabo still wearing lipstick?" I quietly asked Take-san. Take-san began the rubdown and said, "Wiping and washing it off were so chaotic. Although they were all told to remove it, it was too much. They're still young."

"Take-san's job is formidable."

"The director has warned us many times before. He also listened to today's broadcast from the office and was pleased. 'Who proposed today's broadcast? Was it Skylark's invention? As I've said what a delightful child,' said a laughing director, who never smiles," said Take-san who had also been little stirred up by today's lipstick incident and was more talkative than usual.

"It wasn't my invention." It must be viewed as the consequence of a military exploit.

"It's the same thing. If Skylark doesn't say it, I don't act. Didn't I take on the hated role by choice?"

"Hated?"

"Yes," she nodded with her characteristically cool smiling face, "I didn't hate it, but it was hard."

"Peahen's announcement hurt me a little, too."

"Yes, Makita-san...asked to make the announcement. She's a guileless, good person. She's not good at applying make-up. Even I wear a little lipstick, do you understand?"

"So you're equally at fault?"

"It's all right if you don't understand," she calmly said while never stopping the rubdown.

"What a woman," I thought. When I first came to the Dojo, I thought Take-san was cute. She's a sea bream who can't be made a fool.

Well, what do you think? I'm asking you again to visit the Dojo. There is just one venerable woman. If she is not mine, she is not yours. She is a singular treasure, the pride of Japan throughout the world. The praise is a little exaggerated, and I'm embarrassed. At any rate, aren't young women who inspire affection without sex appeal few in number? You should not have any sexual attraction to Take-san. It may be solely feelings of affection. This is a win for us, the New Men. We understand that a friendship of only trust and affection between a man and a woman is possible. This is the natural delicious fruit savored only by the so-called New Man. If you desire this pure delicious fruit, the young poet should visit the Dojo.

Perhaps, you are already savoring an astounding pure fruit near you.

October 20

12

———

KASHOU SENSEI

1

I was so happy you came to visit yesterday. Again thanks for the flowers. And thanks for the little red English dictionaries you gave to Take-san and Mabo. You are indeed a poet. Thank you so much for your kind thoughts, and particularly for bringing gifts for Take-san and Mabo.

They have given me a cigarette case and a bamboo Fuji Musume doll. But I was a little embarrassed and wondered whether I should give them something in return. I was a little worried. I was relieved when you wisely brought gifts. You, more than I, seem to have a newer side. I have received gifts from and given gifts to women, but it bothered me a bit. It's improper. That part of me is a little old-fashioned. I should strive to simply exchange gifts without embarrassment like you. I feel like you just taught me one more thing. I caught a glimpse of your refreshing virtue.

When Mabo said, "You have a guest," and showed you to my room, my heart was beating so fast, like it was hemorrhaging. You understand, don't you? I was so happy to see you after such a long time. More than that, the sight of you and Mabo laughing like old friends as you walked side by side was amazing. I felt like I was in a fairy tale. I only felt that way once before, last spring.

I came down with pneumonia last spring around the time of the high school graduation, and high fever made me groggy. When I happened to look up from the pillow of my sickbed, my head teacher in high school, Kimura Sensei, and my mother were laughingly chatting about something. I was scared to death at that time. They lived in totally different worlds in my school and in my home. Mysteriously, from my pillow, I could see them chatting like old friends. My heart leaped with joy like in some crazy, mixed up fairy tale, or like I had discovered Fuji at Lake Towada.

"You look much better," you said and handed me the flowers. I was at a loss, but unfazed and with total ease, you asked Mabo,

"Do you have an old vase Skylark could borrow?" Mabo nodded and brought one. I seemed to be living in a dream.

I didn't know what was what.

I blurted out the clumsy question, "Have you met Mabo before?"

"Haven't I met her in your letters?"

"That's true."

Then we roared with laughter.

"Did you immediately recognize Mabo?"

"I knew her the moment I laid eyes on her. She was much nicer than I expected."

"How?"

"She's stubborn, but fascinating. She's not as uncouth as I expected. She's like a child."

"So she is."

"But she's not bad and seems delicate."

"That's true."

I felt great.

2

Mabo brought back a slender white vase.

You thanked her and randomly put the flowers in, then said, "Have Take-san rearrange them for you later."

Now, that was a little wrong of you. But you immediately took the small dictionary from your pocket and gave it to Mabo. She didn't look too happy and, without a word, politely bowed and speedily left the room. That is proof that Mabo was offended. Mabo is not the kind of person who stiffly bows politely. It's no use because anyone other than Take-san is no problem at all to you.

"The weather's nice today, so let's go to the balcony on the second floor and talk. It's the noon rest time so it would be okay."

"I learned everything from your letters. You usually go there after the noon rest period. Since today's Sunday, there will also be a tranquility broadcast."

Laughing, we left my room and went upstairs. We suddenly tensed up and discussed the state of the world. I wonder why. Our lives have already been entrusted to the nobility. We can be ready to fly anywhere under orders. Although we had nothing to talk about, we were excited and expressed our innermost thoughts on the so-called rebuilding of the new Japan. No matter how close a relationship guys have, when they meet after a long time, they will have high-minded discussions. Each may be anxious for the other to recognize his own progress. After going out on the balcony, you were angry about Japan starting mediocre elementary education.

"Unfortunately, the kind of education a person receives as a child determines his entire life. I think more elite persons should be provided."

"People who only think about their pay are worthless."

"You're right, absolutely right. Skillful advances are not expected with tricks of practicality. The adults already bargain too much."

"Definitely. The superficial claptrap is old. Shouldn't there be transparency?"

You're as unskilled at debating as I am. We keep saying the same things over and over.

Our bumbling debate gradually filled with gaps. Too many phrases like "simply" or "in summary" or "at any rate" popped up and dragged down the discussion. Around that time, Take-san appeared on the lawn in front of the entrance below.

"Take-san!" I yelled without thinking. At that moment, you straightened your pants. Why did you do that? Take-san raised her right hand to her forehead and looked up at the balcony.

"What?" she said while laughing. At that time, Take-san's figure didn't look so bad.

"A person who really likes Take-san is here right now."

"Stop it. Cut it out," you said. In fact, at that time, the only words that came out were "Stop it. Cut it out." I have also had that experience.

3

"You're horrible!" said Take-san. She then tilted her head at least forty-five degrees to the side and said while laughing, "Welcome," to you. You turned beet red, quickly nodded, and mumbled, "She's...she's beautiful. You fooled me. You wrote that she was tall and an imposing noble woman. So I had no difficulty praising her, she's a beauty."

"Not what you expected?"

As you gushed, "Very, very different. Since you said things like imposing and noble, you fooled me. If she is slim, that must be described. For color, not so black. I'm no good for a beautiful woman like that. It's dangerous," Take-san bowed slightly and went over to the old building.

While searching your pockets then pulling out the small dictionary, you hurriedly said, "Hey, call Take-san back. I have a gift for her."

When I shouted, "Take-san!" to call her back, you said, "If it's okay, I could toss it to you. It's from Skylark, not me." Then you tossed the cute dictionary with the red cover. You were brilliant. I secretly admired you. Take-san deftly caught your fine gift.

The "Thank you so much" she said was directed at you. Despite what you said, Take-san knew that the gift was from you. You sighed as we watched her figure walk to the old building.

"She's dangerous. That one is dangerous," you muttered solemnly. That made me laugh.

"She's dangerous? You could be alone with her in a dark room and you'd be okay. I've already taken that test."

"You're missing the point," you said as if you pitied me.

"Can you tell a beautiful woman from a plain one?"

I resented that question. You tend to misunderstand things. If you view Take-san as being so beautiful, that is the beauty of Take-san's heart, which reflects onto your pure heart. When you look at her objectively, Take-san is not a beautiful woman at all. Now, Mabo is far more beautiful. The brilliance of Take-san's character is the only beauty you see in her. As for a woman's features, I possess a far better sense of beauty than you. At that time, however, I considered the discussion of a woman's looks to be crude, so I said nothing. If you decide on Take-san, we will be at odds and things are apt to get a little awkward. That's not good. Please believe me. Take-san is not a beautiful woman. There's nothing dangerous about her. Dangerous is a joke, right? Take-san is simply an honest, reliable person, like you.

We stood on the balcony for a while without saying a word. Suddenly, the talk of Take-san evaporated when you blurted out that my neighbor Echigo Lion is the famous poet Ootsuki Kashou.

4

"What?!" I said as if in a dream.

"Well, he looks a lot like him. I realized it when I caught a glimpse of him earlier. All of my older brothers were his fans. I've seen many photos of his face since I was little. I was also a fan of his poetry. You know their names?"

"I know them."

Although I'm bad at poetry, I know the poems *Red Star Lilly* and *Seagull* by Ootsuki Kashou so well, I could recite them by heart right now. I can't believe that the author of those poems and I have been sleeping in neighboring beds for several months. I don't know a lot about poems, but as you know, I can safely say that my respect for gifted poets is second to none.

"That man...," I was momentarily overcome by emotion.

"Well, I'm not absolutely sure," you said a little upset, "I only caught a glimpse of him."

At any rate, you had to get a better look. The Sunday tranquility broadcast was coming up soon, so we went downstairs to the Sakura Room. Echigo was asleep. That wasn't a good time to get a good look at him. But we looked at the sleeping lion anyway. We looked at each other and silently nodded in agreement. We both sighed deeply. Anxious, we could not speak. Standing with our backs to the window, the only sound we heard was the record broadcast. The program continued. Finally, when the special attraction of the day, the assistants singing the two-part chorus *Orleans Girl*, began, you poked your right elbow hard into my side.

"That song was written by Kashou Sensei," you whispered excitedly, but I also remembered. When I was a boy, that song was introduced with illustrations in a boys' magazine as a masterpiece by Kashou Sensei. It was very popular. We furtively scrutinized Echigo's face. Until then, Echigo had been lying on his back on his bed with his eyes lightly closed. But when the chorus of *Orleans Girl* began, he opened his eyes, lifted his head from the pillow, and carefully listened. But soon, he wearily shut his eyes again. And with his eyes shut, he let out a sad, weak laugh. You made a fist with your right hand and made a peculiar gesture like punching the air, then sought to shake my hand. Without laughing, we vigorously shook hands. Thinking about that now, what was that handshake for? I don't get it, but at that time, we couldn't be still and settle down. We were too excited.

When *Orleans Girl* ended, your mysteriously hoarse voice said, "Well, we should go." I nodded and sent you out to the hall and followed.

Then in unison we shouted, "It's him!"

5

Of course, you know all of this, but after leaving you and returning alone to my room, my feelings surpassed excitement, I was so scared the blood drained from my face. I deliberately laid down on my back so I couldn't see Echigo. I felt a queer mixture of anxiety, fear, and edginess, and couldn't calm down. It became unbearable. In a soft voice, I finally said, "Kashou Sensei!"

He said nothing. Boldly, I jerked my head around to face Kashou Sensei. Echigo had silently begun his stretching and bending exercises. I hurriedly began exercising. I spread my legs and arms far apart, and while I slowly folded in the fingers of each hand starting from the pinky, I asked with an unexpected calm, "Do you think they sang that song not knowing who wrote it?"

"It's best to forget about the writer," he calmly replied. I finally had no doubt that this man was Kashou Sensei.

"Forgive me for not recognizing you before. When my friend told me earlier was the first time I knew. My friend and I have loved your poems since we were boys."

"Thank you," he said seriously, "but Echigo had been carefree until now."

"Why don't you write poems anymore?"

"Times have changed," he said and laughed.

My heart stopped, and I couldn't think of a thing to say. We exercised in silence for a while. Without warning, an angry Echigo abruptly said, "Stop bothering people! Lately, you have been insolent!" I was startled. Echigo had never snapped at me. It would be best if I promptly apologized.

"I'm sorry. I won't say anymore."

"Yes, don't say a word. You guys don't get it. You know nothing."

It had become very uncomfortable. Poets are scary. I'm not sure what I did that was so rude. Not one word passed between us the rest of the day. The assistants came for the rubdown and tried to chat with me a few times, but I only pouted and never responded. In my heart, I was itching to surprise Mabo by telling her that Echigo actually wrote *Orleans Girl*. But Echigo saying, "Don't say a word," muzzled me. Well, I had no choice. Last night, I cried myself to sleep.

Serendipitously, this morning, I was able to easily reconcile with Kashou Sensei, who I had enraged. Echigo's daughter came to visit him this morning for the first time in a long time. Kiyoko-san, his daughter, is about the same age as Mabo. She's a small, thin, gentle woman with a bad complexion and slanted eyes. She arrived right in the middle of breakfast. As she was untying a large bundle she brought, she said to her father, "I made some pickled seaweed for you."

"Oh good. I should have some now. Take it out...and please give half to Skylark over there."

"What?" I thought. Until now, Echigo, the teacher, had only addressed me as Oshiba-kun, his student, and, oddly enough, never by the more personal and intimate, Skylark.

6

She brought the pickled seaweed over to me.

"Do you have a container I could put it in?"

"Yes...no...," I said a little flustered while getting off the bed, "There on the shelf."

"Here?" she asked as she squatted down and took the anodized aluminum lunch box off the lower shelf of my bed.

"Yes, yes. Thank you."

As she crouched down beside my bed and put the pickled seaweed into the lunch box, she asked, "Would you like to eat it now?"

"No, thank you. Breakfast is over."

She put the lunch box back on the shelf and stood up.

"Oh, they're so pretty," she said, praising those chrysanthemum flowers you dumped in the vase. You said that I should have Take-san arrange them, but when I asked her, she became embarrassed. When I asked Mabo, she forced herself but unintentionally left the flowers unchanged.

"Yesterday, my friend dropped them in there. No one would arrange them for me."

In a glance, she assessed Echigo's mood as he picked his teeth with a toothpick after finishing his meal, and smiling said, "I'll arrange them for you."

I'm in a great mood this morning, but I'm not feeling too good.

Echigo's daughter blushed and hesitantly approached my bedside. She removed all of the chrysanthemums from the vase, then started to put each one back. What a nice person to arrange them for me, I was overjoyed.

Echigo sat cross-legged on his bed enjoying the flower arranging skills of his daughter.

"Maybe I should write poems again," he muttered.

I didn't want to yell out something stupid, so I kept my mouth shut.

"Skylark, I apologize for yesterday," he said, furtively nodding.

"Oh, no, I'm sorry for being so brash."

Out of nowhere, we reconciled.

"Maybe I should write poems again," he repeated.

"Please write. Please write for us. We would really love to read light, honest poems like yours. I'm no expert, but we are searching for art like the music of Mozart, art that is exuberant and radiates goodness. Strangely affected gestures and grave seriousness are already old and obvious. Are there any poets to eloquently recite even in the small green patches in the corners of the ruins of a fire? It's not to escape reality. The hardships are all too obvious. I already intend to live with indifference. It is not an escape. Life is on hold. It's carefree. We feel that now the truth resides only in art with the touch of a swiftly running, clear stream to exactly match our feelings. I'm the type who doesn't need a life or a name. If I weren't, I think I would not be able to ride out this crisis. Watch the birds flying through the air. It's not a matter of doctrines, the *-isms*. Those things are deceptive and useless. I understand the degree of purity of a person, by only his touch. The problem is the touch. It is the rhythm. If no goodness is radiated, everyone is a fraud."

I tried my best to express my weak reasoning. When I finished, I felt embarrassed and thought that I should have kept my mouth shut.

7

"Has it come to that?" asked Kashou Sensei, wiping the tip of his nose with a towel and lying down on his back, "At least, you should leave here soon."

"Yes. Yes."

Ever since I came to the Dojo, I've been secretly impatient to quickly get well. It's a waste, but the sea lane in the heavens felt sluggish.

"You fellows are different," he said and seemed, as expected, to be keenly sensitive to my feelings, "Don't be impatient. If you calm down and live here, you will certainly get well. Then you can aptly play a role in rebuilding Japan." He started to say, "I'm already old...," but his daughter had finished arranging the flowers.

Instead he cheerfully said, "It's worse than before!"

Fuming, she approached his bed and whispered, "Father! All you do is complain. That's why you're so unpopular."

"My thoughts are not allowed in the world?" said Echigo very sadly, but chuckling.

I had completely forgotten the irritation about the earlier blunders. I was ecstatic and grinning.

Without a doubt, a new age is coming. It will be light like a robe of feathers and will be cool and clear like a shallow stream flowing over white sand. In high school, Priest Fukuda taught us that Basho called the waning years of life *karumi*, lightness; which he placed far above *wabi*, simple and quiet; *sabi*, elegant simplicity; and *shiori*, sensitivity to nature and humanity. We are unable to boast with pride of quickly and naturally achieving that advanced state of mind masters like Basho foresaw and aspired to late in their lives. This *karumi* is nothing like frivolity. If desire and life are not abandoned, I don't understand this frame of mind. It is a gust of wind that comes after strenuously working and being soaked with sweat. It is a bird so light that its wings are transparent and is born from

99

the air of difficulties in the maelstrom of the world. Those who don't understand this will probably be excluded, like residue, from the flow of history forever. That will slowly age, and this will slowly age. And you will have no reasons, nothing. The peace of mind of one who has lost everything and has abandoned everything is *karumi*.

This morning, I gave an inept discourse on art to Echigo and was chagrined. But Echigo's daughter became a secret supporter of us and gave me considerable confidence to talk big here as a New Man, and I tried to add to the previous theory.

By the way, your reputation at the Dojo is outstanding. The mood is very good. You just visited the Dojo, and I'm not exaggerating when I say that the atmosphere of the Dojo instantly brightened. The clock has been turned back ten years for Kashou Sensei. Both Take-san and Mabo send their regards.

Mabo's reason is "He has nice eyes. He seems to be a genius. His eyelashes are long and when he blinks you can hear them slapping together." She tends to exaggerate. It's best not to believe her. Shall I tell you Take-san's comment? Please listen calmly without judgment.

"He's a fitting challenge for Skylark."

That's it. However, she did blush when she said it. Bye.

October 29

13

TAKE-SAN

1

Greetings,

Today, I have some sad news. I say sad, but it's a sweet sadness. Take-san is getting married. Who is she marrying? The director. She's going to marry Dr. Tajima, the director of The Health Dojo. I heard this from Mabo today.

I'll start at the beginning.

This morning, my mother came to the Dojo to bring clothes and a few other things. She comes twice a month and arranges my stuff. She took one look at me and, as always, teasingly said, "You're a little homesick, aren't you?"

"Perhaps," I deliberately lied, as always.

"When I leave today, someone should see me off as far as Little Plum Bridge."

"Who?"

"Well, you."

"Me? Can I go out? Do I have permission?"

She nodded and said, "Well, if you are not up to it, is there anyone who could?"

"Not up to it? I have walked ten miles in one day."

"Perhaps," said my mother, mimicking me.

It's been four months since I've taken off my nightclothes and put on my kimono with the splash pattern. When my mother and I went out to the entryway, the director was standing there in silence with both hands clasped behind his back.

"Is he able to walk? Is it all right?" asked my mother as if she were talking to herself and smiling.

"Your son could stand and walk since he was a year old," said the director, his feeble attempt at humor, "I'll have an assistant accompany you."

Mabo emerged from the office wearing a white nurse's uniform and a short *haori* coat with a red camellia flower pattern and jogged over to us. A nervous Mabo bowed awkwardly to my mother. Our chaperone would be Mabo.

I put on my new wooden clogs and went straight out. The clogs were strangely heavy and I stumbled. "Ah, the toddler is very good," joked the director from behind me. His tone was filled with a cold, strong will rather than affection. I felt like he was scolding me, "Very sloppy!" I was disheartened. Without turning around, I briskly took five or six more steps. Again from behind, the director sternly called out, "Start slowly. Start slowly," but this time I felt a kind affection in his words.

I walked slowly. My mother and Mabo followed while chatting in whispers to each other. When we passed through the pine grove and onto the paved prefectural road, I felt a little lightheaded and stood still.

"It's big. The road is so big."

The paved road shone dully under the soft rays of autumn light, but for a moment, it appeared to me as a vast and chaotic river.

"Is this too much?" asked my smiling mother, "What should we do? Should you see me off the next time?"

2

"I'm okay. I'm okay," I said and intentionally slapped my clogs hard as I walked. Just as I said, "I'm used to them now," a truck flew past me with tremendous force and, without thinking, I squealed.

My mother immediately mocked me, "It's big. The truck is so big."

"It's not that big, but it's powerful. Amazing horsepower. Definitely about 100,000 HP."

"Well, what about today's atomic trucks?" My mother was in a great mood that morning.

We leisurely walked on. As we neared the bus stop at Little Plum Bridge, I heard something totally unexpected. The chat between my mother and Mabo that had covered various matters ended with, "I heard that the director is getting married soon."

"Yes. Very soon to Takenaka-san."

"Takenaka-san? Oh, the assistant," said my mother, she seemed surprised. I was one hundred times more surprised, shocked, like I had been run over by a 100,000-HP atomic truck. My mother soon regained her composure, smiled and said, "Takenaka-san is a fine woman. The director is a discerning man." She inquired no further and gently turned the conversation to other matters.

I don't clearly recall what shape I was in when my mother departed at the bus stop. Everything was a blur, and my heart pounded as if it were leaping out of my chest. The feeling was unbearable.

I have a confession. I like Take-san. I liked her from the start. Mabo wasn't the problem. I thought I could somehow forget about Take-san by getting closer to Mabo. I tried really hard to like Mabo, but it was no good. In my letters to you, I only recounted Mabo's beauty and often criticized Take-san. I wasn't trying to deceive you, I wrote those things because I wanted to erase my feelings. When the New Man thinks about Take-san, his body becomes weighed down and his wings wither. He worries that he has become a trivial man like a pig's tail. Simple feelings are revealed on the face of the New Man. He wanted to become totally indifferent to Take-san. My heart and I tried our best. We did. Could you, who saw Take-san as simply a good person, a sea bream, and a bad shopper, have a little sympathy for my anguish about my bad-mouthing? My secret hope was if you supported me and joined in bad-mouthing Take-san, maybe I would tire of her and be free, but that didn't happen. You were captivated by Take-san, and I was ruined. Then I changed tactics and openly praised Take-san. I plotted to trap you in a new model of companionship between a man and a woman, a friendship without sexual attraction. These are the sad facts of the events so far. Far from having no sexual attraction, I had a lot. I was in a wretched state of wild passion.

3

You said that Take-san is a great beauty, and I heatedly denied that, but I do think that Take-san is a beautiful woman. I thought so the first time I saw her on the day I arrived at the Dojo.

To you, a woman like Take-san is a truly beautiful woman. In an extraordinary sign immediately before daybreak in the depths of darkness, Take-san crouched down wiping the floor boards in the washroom under the hazy glow of the blue light bulb was terrifyingly beautiful. I'm a good loser, but I had to endure. If it had been anyone else, a crime definitely would have been committed. Crazy Legs often says, "A woman is a demon." Without realizing it, a woman may temporarily lose her humanity and become an enchantress.

Now, I will confess. I love Take-san. The old and the new don't exist.

When my mother left, my knees trembled as I walked and I developed an unbearable thirst. I said, "Can I rest a little somewhere?" My voice was so hoarse I thought it was my father's, and I felt like the words were being muttered by someone far away.

"You seem tired. We'll go a little further. There's a place where we can rest."

Guided by Mabo, I entered what looked like a pre-world war Miyoshino-style building. A broken bicycle and charcoal sacks were strewn about the wide, dimly lit dirt floor. One crude table and a couple of chairs were placed in a corner. A large mirror hung on the wall beside the table and glowed a striking, eerie white light. This house is used for business and a place where close friends can enjoy some tea. Sometimes the assistants from the Dojo go there to buy oil. Mabo strolled in and returned with an earthenware teapot of cheap tea and teacups. We sat down facing each other at the table below the mirror and drank the warm tea. I sighed deeply and felt a little better.

I managed to casually asked, "So Take-san is getting married."

"Yes," said Mabo looking sad for some reason. She narrowed her shoulders, as if protecting herself from the cold, looked straight at me and asked, "Didn't you know?"

"No," I said as my eyes suddenly teared up. I quickly looked down.

"I understand. Take-san cried."

"I don't want to say anything about it," said Mabo like it was a secret; she was disgusted and angry.

"Don't say something foolish."

"It's not foolish," said Mabo tearing up, "So I won't say a thing. I must stay friends with Take-san."

"Don't stay friends. You have to say what you know. You have no other choice. Take-san's getting married is a good thing. Isn't it something to be happy about?"

"No. I know, but deception is wrong." The tears flowing from her eyes collected in her eyelashes and fell in large drops onto her cheeks.

"I know. I know."

4

"Stop. It doesn't make sense?" I said. It's hard to have someone look at you in a situation like this.

"What doesn't make sense?" she asked. When I heard my words again, I didn't believe they made much sense.

"Skylark, you're so easygoing," Mabo said laughing slightly while using her index finger to wipe the tears off her cheeks, "You didn't know about the director and Take-san until now."

"Not a thing about that disgusting affair." I immediately felt awful and wanted to fight the world.

"What's disgusting? Is marriage disgusting?"

"No, that's not it," I mumbled, "Did something happen..."

"No not that. It's not like that. The director is a respectable man. Without saying a word to Take-san, he went and asked permission from her father. He had been evacuated to this area. Then Take-san's father spoke to her. She cried for two or three nights. Her becoming a bride is dreadful."

"In that case, it's all right," I said relieved.

"Why is it all right? Was crying all right? That's horrible, Skylark," she said with a smile. She tilted her head to the side, looked at me with those bright eyes, and extended her right hand and squeezed my hand resting on the table.

"You see, Take-san loves you, Skylark. That's why she cried," she said and squeezed even harder. For some unknown reason, I squeezed back. It was a meaningless grip. I instantly felt stupid and pulled my hand back.

"Do you want another cup?" I asked trying to hide my embarrassment.

"No," said Mabo. She lowered her eyes and seemed timid. Her decisive refusal was a mysterious refusal.

"Shall we go?"

"Yes."

She gave a small nod and raised her head. Her face was lovely. Absolutely lovely. On her expressionless face, fine lines from fatigue had appeared on the sides of her nose, her mouth was open just a bit. Her pale face had such elegance with those large, cold, deep clear eyes. This elegance is possessed by people who have let go of everything. Mabo chose to suffer, and, for the first time, had become a selfless woman who revealed a new beauty. She is one of us. She has yielded to the huge newly-built ship and is innocently advancing in the sea lane of the heavens. The faint winds of hope brushed her cheeks. The beauty of Mabo's face surprised me, and the phrase "the eternal maiden" came to mind. Those usually grandiose sounding words were not the least bit grandiose at that time. They felt fresh and new. A lout like me using the refined words "the eternal maiden" may amuse you, but, at that time, I was saved by Mabo's noble features.

I already thought of Take-san's marriage as an event far in the past and felt like a weight had been lifted. It wasn't a conscious action, as if I had given up, but felt like the scene before my eyes was instantly far away, similar to looking through the wrong end of a telescope. Nothing troubled my heart. I was left with a refreshing feeling of satisfaction, like everything was complete.

5

American planes circled the clear blue sky of late fall. We stood in front of the Miyoshino-style building and looked up at them.

"They're flying around in vain."

"Yeah," Mabo said with a smile.

"But the planes have a new elegant shape. Not one unnecessary ornament."

"Yes," said Mabo softly and watched the planes fly off through the sky with a childlike innocence.

"A form with no unneeded ornaments is nice."

Not only the planes, but the gentle form of Mabo's distracted look left a peaceful impression.

We continued to walk without talking. I thought that from now on I will carefully look at the faces of women I encounter, and to some degree, the innocent, transparent beauty of Mabo will appear in all of their faces. Women have become womanly. But the change is not in the women before the world war. The new womanliness has experienced the suffering of war. How can I say this? You could probably understand if I said their beauty echoes the song of a bush warbler, the lightness.

We arrived back at the Dojo a little before noon. We had walked more than 1 ¼ miles. I was so tired I just fell into bed and slept without even changing into my nightclothes or taking off my coat.

"Skylark, lunchtime."

I barely opened my eyes and saw Take-san standing there with a tray and smiling.

Ah, the director's bride!

I jumped right up and, as I bowed a little without thinking, said, "Oh! Excuse me."

"You're sleepy. Sleepyhead," she said as if talking to herself and set the tray by the head of my bed.

"Some people sleep in their clothes, but take care to not catch a cold this time of year. It's best to quickly change into your night-clothes," she said crossly with a frown as she took the nightclothes out of my bed drawer.

"Take care of yourself. Here, I'll help you change."

I got out of bed and untied my belt. Same old Take-san. I started to think that this marriage to the director was a lie. I was still asleep and dreaming. I instantly rejoiced, my mother's visit was a dream, and Mabo's crying at the building, a dream. But none of that was true.

What lovely Kurume-gasuri cloth," remarked Take-san as she made me get out of my kimono, "You look quite handsome in it Skylark. Mabo's a lucky girl. So...on the way back, you two had tea at Auntie's place."

It wasn't a dream after all.

"Congratulations Take-san," I said.

She did not answer. She silently tied the belt behind me, then she shoved her hand up the sleeve of my nightclothes and sharply pinched my armpit. I gritted my teeth to endure the pain.

6

I changed into my nightclothes as if nothing had happened and started to eat. Beside me, Take-san folded my kimono. Not a word passed between us. After a short time, Take-san, barely audible, muttered, "Patience."

That word appeared to sum up all of Take-san's thoughts.

"What a horrible guy," I whispered trying to mimic Take-san's accent as I continued eating.

Those words seemed to sum up all of my thoughts.

Take-san burst out laughing and said, "Thank you very much."

We had reconciled. I wanted to pray with all my heart for Take-san's happiness.

"How much longer will you be here?"

"The rest of this month."

"Will you have a farewell party?"

"I hope not!"

She feigned a chill running through her, quickly put away the kimono and left the room looking unconcerned. All of the people around me are this wonderful.

I'm writing this letter while listening to the 1 pm lecture. Today's topic is.... Who do you think is broadcasting? Can you guess? You'll be happy to hear that it's Ootsuki Kashou Sensei. Ootsuki Sensei's popularity around the Dojo has soared. His crass nickname Echigo Lion has been retired. For two or three days after you discovered him, I told no one with much difficulty. But finally I told Mabo in confidence. The rumor spread in a flash. He was unconditionally revered as the composer of *Orleans Girl*. When the director made his rounds, he apologized to Kashou Sensei for not previously knowing.

Students in the annex, of course, and in the old building rushed with requests for corrections to poems, tanka, and haiku verses. However, Kashou Sensei did not display an ounce of arrogance or thoughtlessness, and was, after all, the reserved Echigo Lion. He left correcting the students' works mostly to Crazy Legs. Crazy Legs was in his glory. He intended to become Kashou Sensei's top disciple. He assumed a more serious expression and corrected the works painstakingly created by the others as he pleased. Today, at the request of the administration, Kashou Sensei will lecture for the first time. His topic is *Devotion*. As I hear his voice flowing out of the speakers, I am inspired being taught by such a venerable man. His voice possesses a quiet dignity. Kashou Sensei may be a greater man than I thought. The speech is excellent, not the least bit out of date.

Devotion is nothing like mindlessly killing oneself with hopeless sentimentality. There is an immense difference. Devotion is to live a worthwhile life forever. Humanity is immortal only by relying on this pure devotion. However, there is no need to dress up for devotion. Today, I should offer everything as I am. The plowman should show devotion as the field hand with the plow. You cannot be an impostor. You're not allowed to postpone devotion. Every moment of life must have devotion. He often stressed the absolute meaninglessness of devising an ingenious plan on how to act with complete devotion. I blushed many times while listening. Even now, I announce, "I'm a New Man. I'm a New Man," a little too often. I adorned my devotion too elaborately. I think the nitpicking about the make-up was an example. I should bravely take down the billboard of The New Man around here. My surroundings are becoming as bright as I am. Until now, usually, haven't the places we appeared automatically become bright and splendid? After that, there is nothing more to say. We will move straight ahead at the perfect pace, neither too fast nor too slow. Where does this road lead? Perhaps, you should ask a growing vine. The vine may answer, "I don't know. But I grow toward the sunlight."

So long.

December 9

GOODBYE

PROLOGUE

An elder of mine translated the five-character Chinese poem 人生足别离 in the *Book of Songs* as "Life is only goodbyes." Indeed, the joy felt upon meeting vanishes in an instant, but the pain of separation runs deep. It is no exaggeration to say that we always live with a reluctance to part.

Goodbye is an exaggeration of the phases of parting between modern gentlemen and ladies, but hopefully, the myriad of phases in these partings is depicted.

1

A CHANGE OF MIND - 1

The rain began as the funeral for the old literary master came to a close. It was an early spring rain.

Two men departed walking under a shared umbrella. Both were indebted to the late master. They talked about his indiscretions with women. The middle-aged man of importance wearing a garment bearing a family crest was a writer. The much younger man wearing [Harold] Lloyd glasses and a pinstripe suit was an editor.

The writer said, "Like you, he was quite fond of the ladies. It will soon be your day of reckoning? You look exhausted."

The editor blushed and replied, "I intend to leave them all."

The writer always spoke in blunt and vulgar terms. For a long time, the handsome editor had kept his distance, but today he had forgotten his umbrella. He had no choice, but to share the writer's umbrella and get an earful.

He did intend to leave them all. That was not a total lie.

Change has come. Three years have passed since the war ended, and things have changed.

Tajima Shuji, the thirty-four year old editor of the magazine *Obelisk*, speaks with a hint of a Kansai accent, but rarely talks about his hometown. This savvy fellow edits *Obelisk* and manufactures its appearance to the world. In fact, he aids the black market and is always flush with cash. But it was easy come, easy go. The rumor is that he drinks enough liquor to drown in and has ten or so lovers.

However, he is not single. Not only is he not single, his current wife is his second wife. His first wife died of pneumonia and left a dimwitted little girl. He sold his house in Tokyo and evacuated to a friend's home in Saitama Prefecture. During that time, he married his current wife. Of course, this was her first marriage. Her farming family doesn't look it, but they are well off.

When the war ended, his wife and little girl were living with her parents. He went alone to Tokyo and rented a one-room apartment in a suburb. He was shrewd. The room was just a place to sleep. He was often out and about which allowed him to save quite a lot.

But over the three years, his feelings have changed. At times, his feelings resembled homesickness. He wondered if the fault lies in the subtle changes that have occurred in the world, or the recent emaciation of his body due to his daily excesses. No, no, it was simply getting older. All was vanity. He had tired of drinking. He would buy a small house and summon his wife and child in the country to join him. But just as quickly, those feelings would pass.

Perhaps, this time he would break away from the black market and devote himself to editing the magazine. But...

There was an obstacle. First, he had to skillfully break up with the women. When he thought about it, this clever man was stumped and could only sigh.

"You intend to break up with all of them...," said the eminent writer who then screwed up his mouth in a wry smile and said, "That's fine, but you seem to have quite a few."

2

A CHANGE OF MIND - 2

Tajima looked to be on the verge of tears. The more he thought about it, he realized that he had neither the strength nor the ability to do it alone. If he tried to pay them off without a reason, he didn't believe the women would back off.

"Thinking about it now, I probably look insane. Unbelievably, they may welcome it..."

The idea crossed his mind to confess everything to this middle-aged hack writer and get his advice.

"I hate to surprise people with praise. However, women may prefer a passionate fellow who is strangely adverse to morality. If you are young, good looking, have money, and moreover, are tolerant in terms of morals, you'll be popular. That's to be expected. Although you intend to leave them, they won't agree to it."

"That's true."

The editor wiped his face with a handkerchief.

"Are you crying?" asked the writer.

"No, the rain has clouded the lenses of my glasses...."

"Well, your voice sounds like you're crying. A hopeless ladies' man."

As the writer pointed out, Tajima served the black market, was amoral, and had a strange faithfulness to women. For that reason, women seemed to rely deeply on Tajima without the least apprehension.

"You don't have a good plan, do you?" asked the editor, "No. Maybe you should go overseas for five or six years, but traveling to the West isn't so easy these days. You should call all those women to a room and make them sing *Auld Lang Syne*. No. Better yet, *Aogeba Totoshi* [Respect Your Teacher]. Then hand each one a diploma, act like you've gone mad, leap outside stark naked, and run away. That should do it. The women should be thoroughly disgusted and ditch you."

Completely worthless advice.

"Excuse me, but my train is over there..."

"Not yet. Walk with me to the next stop. You have a big problem. We will figure this out together."

The writer appeared to be bored that day and wouldn't let Tajima leave."

"No, that's okay. I can..."

"No, no. You can't solve this alone. You'll probably kill yourself. I'm actually worried. Being in love with a woman and dying is not drama, it's comedy. No, it's farce. It's hilarious. No one has an ounce of sympathy. Death isn't an option. Hmm...I've got it. Find a stunningly beautiful woman somewhere and explain your situation to her. Then have her pretend to be your wife as you visit each of your women. The effect will be immediate. All of the women will back off. Why don't you try it?"

A thin straw for a drowning man. Tajima started to come around just a little.

3

THE MARCH - 1

Tajima decided to give it a try. However, there remained one problem.

The stunningly beautiful woman. If she were plain looking, he would encounter about thirty every time he walked a few blocks to the train stop. He doubted a stunningly beautiful woman even existed outside of fairy tales.

Tajima had always been proud of his looks, stylish, and incredibly vain. When he walked with a homely woman, he would escape by claiming a sudden stomachache. All of his current lovers were nice looking, but none could be said to be stunningly beautiful.

On that rainy day, that random chatter from the middle-aged hack writer provided a "secret." Despite being temporarily repulsed by its absurdity, Tajima felt it had the seed of a good plan.

He would try it. That stunningly beautiful woman may have been dropped into some corner of life. His eyes suddenly began to dart around nervously behind his glasses.

The dance halls. The cafes. The lounges. Not there, not there. Only homely ones. Offices, department stores, factories, movie theaters, burlesque shows. No one there. He disgracefully skulked around peeking through the fences enclosing the campuses of women's colleges, raced around to the venues of Miss Whatever beauty contests, and under the pretense of a visitor, snuck into the testing rooms for new faces in the cinema. All his wanderings led to no one.

He met his quarry on his way home.

He was dejected as he walked through the black market behind Shinjuku Station at dusk. He had no interest in visiting his so-called lovers. Thinking of them made him shudder. He had to break up with them.

Out of the blue, someone behind him called, "Tajima-san!"

He was startled.

"Um, do I know you?" he asked.

"What...don't you remember?" asked this person in a horrible voice resembling a squawking crow.

"Uh...?" he said looking again. Suddenly, he recognized her.

He knew that woman. She's from the black market, no, she's a street peddler. He had only traded black market goods with her two or three times. Nonetheless, he remembered the raspy voice and the superhuman strength of this woman. Although thin, she could easily haul around eighty pounds on her back. Usually, she smelled of fish and wore muddy clothes. When she was wearing baggy *Monpe* pants and rubber boots, it was hard to tell whether she was a man or a woman. She looked like a beggar. After doing business with her, the dapper Tajima felt compelled to immediately wash his hands.

This improbable Cinderella princess had a refined elegance complimented by Western clothes, a slender build, and lovely small hands and feet. She looked to be twenty-three or -four, no more like twenty-five or -six years old with a face bearing a look of sorrow and a pale complexion, like the flower of a pear. This peddler who could haul eighty pounds was, undoubtedly, a stunningly beautiful woman of nobility.

However, that grating voice was a blemish, he had to make sure she never spoke. He could use her.

4

THE MARCH - 2

They say that the clothes make the man, but a woman, in particular, is transformed for some unknown reason by her dress. She may essentially be a phantom. However, it is rare to find a woman able to transform as brilliantly as this woman called Nagai Kinuko.

"Well, you've stashed a lot away. It's probably hard to get dressed up," he said.

"Yeah. It's hard," she said.

In a flash, that awful voice erased the nobility, all of it.

"I have a favor to ask of you."

"You, the cheapskate who only wants a price cut..."

"No, this is not about business. I intend to wash my hands of that business soon. Are you still always thirsty?"

"Of course. Can't eat my food without a drink," she said inelegantly.

"Is this how you usually dress?" he asked.

"This is my feminine side. Once in a while, I want to dress up and go see a movie."

"What's playing today?"

"Well, I just saw it. It was...let me see...*Ashikurige*..."

"You probably mean *Hizakurige*. Did you go alone?"

"What? No. Men act funny."

"I thought so. I have a request. Do you have an hour, no, thirty minutes to spare?"

"A nice talk?"

"You won't lose any money."

As the two walked side by side, eight out of ten people passing them turned around to look. They weren't looking at Tajima, but at Kinuko. The handsome Tajima was pushed aside by the elegance of Kinuko. In her presence, he appeared trashy and poor.

Tajima guided Kinuko to a familiar dimly lit restaurant.

"What's good here?"

"Uh, well, they're proud of their *tonkatsu*."

"I'll have that. I'm so hungry. And what else is good?"

"Pretty much everything. What do you want to eat?"

"What they're proud of. Is there anything other than tonkatsu?"

"The tonkastu serving here is huge."

"What a tightwad. You're useless. I'll go inside and ask."

She had superhuman strength and was a big eater, but was an exquisitely beautiful woman. He couldn't let her escape.

Tajima drank whiskey as he described his so-called favor while watching Kinuko eat and eat and eat as feelings of hatred welled up in him. As Kinuko ate, maybe she was listening or maybe she wasn't, but she seemed to have lost interest in his story.

"Will you do it?

"You're an idiot. Why not just do nothing?"

5

THE MARCH - 3

Tajima cringed at the unexpected jab from his opponent, "Well, I asked you because I am doing absolutely nothing. I'm in a fix."

"Even without this messy business, when things go bad, you won't see them anymore anyway. That's good."

"I could never behave so outrageously. In the future, those women may get married or find a new lover. The man has the responsibility to correctly assess the feelings of his partners."

"What! A sorry responsibility. You talk about breaking up and still want to have relations? You really look like a lecher."

"Hey! Your rudeness is infuriating. Even rudeness has limits. Why don't you just eat?"

"I wonder if they have *kinton*."

"You're still hungry? Is there something wrong with your stomach? You have some disease. Why don't you have a doctor look at it? You've already eaten quite a lot. You've had enough."

"You really are cheap. It's normal for a woman to eat this much. A young lady who denies herself more is only making herself look good because she's being seductive. Me, I'll eat as much as I can."

"Haven't you had enough? This restaurant isn't cheap. Do you always eat this much?"

"Not at all. Only when someone else is treating."

"So if I'll be feeding you so much from now on, you can at least hear me out."

"But I have to work. I'll lose money."

"I'll pay you separately for that. I'll pay you the amount you usually make."

"So I only have to walk with you?"

"Yes, that's it. But there are two conditions. I ask that you not say a word when the other woman is present. You can only laugh, nod, and shake your head. The other condition is you don't eat in front of them. You may eat as much as you like, but only when it's just you and me. In front of other people, you're allowed one cup of tea."

"And the money? You're cheap. Are you gonna trick me?"

"Don't worry. I'm desperate. If this fails, I'm ruined."

"Okay...you're backing up into a wall."

"What? No...dummy. My back is up against the wall."

"Oh, is that it?" she said completely unconcerned. Tajima was disgusted. But she was beautiful. She had a dignity and elegance inconceivable in this world.

Tonkatsu. Chicken croquette. Tuna sashimi. Squid sashimi. Ramen. Eel. Stew. Grilled skewers of beef. Sushi platter. Shrimp salad. Strawberries and cream.

And she wanted kinton. Isn't a woman, anyone, who eats this much, nauseating?

6

———

THE MARCH - 4

Kinuko's apartment was in the Setagaya district. Since she usually peddled her goods during the morning, she would be free after two in the afternoon. About once a week on a day that was good for both of them, Tajima promised to phone her to arrange a meeting place, and together they would march off to the woman to be dumped.

A few days later, the march of two started toward a beauty parlor in a department store in Nihon-bashi.

The winter before last, a dapper Tajima wandered into the beauty parlor to get a permanent wave. The head hairdresser, Aoki, was a war widow around thirty years old. He didn't try to pick her up because women pursued him. Aoki commuted to work at the store in Nihon-bashi from the store's dormitory in Tsukiji. She barely earned enough to make ends meet. Therefore, Tajima helped with her living expenses. Even now, the relationship between Tajima and Aoki is common knowledge in the dormitory.

However, Tajima was a rare sight at the Nihon-bashi store while Aoki was at work. He thought that frequent appearances of a sophisticated, handsome man like himself would surely interfere with her business.

Nevertheless, he suddenly appeared at her store accompanied by a stunning woman.

"Good afternoon," he greeted her with no hint of intimacy, "Today, I've brought my wife. She had been evacuated and I sent for her."

That was sufficient. Aoki was also a very beautiful woman with her cool eyes, soft white skin, and not one unrefined feature. However, compared to Kinuko, he thought the difference was between silver slippers and combat boots.

The two beautiful women greeted each other in silence. Aoki already looked obsequious and seemed about to cry. It was clear who had won and who had lost.

As was stated earlier, Tajima was conscientious toward women and had never lied by saying he was single. All of the women knew from the beginning that his wife and child had been evacuated to the country. Finally, they had come to live with Tajima. Moreover, that wife was young, noble, cultured, and had no equal in beauty.

Aside from crying, Aoki had no options.

Getting carried away, Tajima finished her off by asking, "Would you please fix my wife's hair? I've heard that nowhere, not even in Ginza, is there a hairdresser as skilled as you."

However, that was not necessarily a compliment. The fact was that there were many excellent, skilled hairdressers.

Kinuko sat down facing the mirror.

As tears were about to spill out, Aoki draped a white cutting cape over Kinuko's shoulders and began combing her hair.

Kinuko was unconcerned.

Tajima, however, bolted from his seat.

7

—————

THE MARCH - 5

When Aoki finished, Tajima quietly entered the salon and slid a wad, a little more than an inch thick, of yen notes into a pocket of the hairdresser's white jacket. With a feeling of supplication, he whispered, "Goodbye."

His voice even astonished him. It seemed to be charged with consideration, apology, kindness, and wistfulness.

Kinuko stood up without saying a word. Also without speaking, Aoki straightened Kinuko's skirt. Tajima flew out before Kinuko.

"Breaking up is painful," he thought.

An expressionless Kinuko followed and said, "That didn't go so good."

"What?"

"The permanent."

He wanted to scream "You Fool!" but held back because they were in the store. The woman Aoki never spoke ill of another. She didn't desire money and kindly did his laundry.

"Well, are we done?"

"Yes."

Tajima still felt miserable.

"With that act, you've managed to break up. That girl's got no guts. She is kind of beautiful, isn't she? With those looks..."

"Stop it! How rude, don't call her 'that girl.' She is a gentle woman. That lady... You're another story. Be quiet. When I hear your grating, crow-like voice, I go mad."

"Oh dear, I'm so very sorry."

Aaah! What a cheap shot. Tajima really seemed to be going mad.

Because of Tajima's strange vanity, when going out with a woman, he would hand over his wallet to her in advance so she would pay. He took on a liberal attitude like he was completely unconcerned about money. However, until now, no woman went shopping on her own without his permission.

But Miss I'm-so-very-sorry shopped with no difficulty. The department store sold some very expensive items. With dignity and without hesitation, she selected luxury goods, more than that, all her selections, naturally, were refined and tasteful.

"Behave yourself. Would you stop it?"

"What a miser."

"Would you like to eat now?"

"Yes. Today I will restrain myself for you."

"Please give back my wallet. Don't spend more than 5,000 yen."

This time, there was no vanity or any other crap.

"I didn't spend that much."

"No, you spent a lot. Later, I'll see how much is left, then I'll know. You definitely spent more than 10,000 yen. Your meal wasn't cheap the other day."

"How about I quit? I get whatever I like, and I walk around with you."

That was a threat.

Tajima could only sigh.

8

SUPERHUMAN STRENGTH - 1

However, Tajima had never been ordinary. He was an astute, clever man who assisted in the black market and could easily reap several tens of thousands of yen in short order.

His character didn't allow him to exploit and throw away Kinuko. In silence, he demonstrated the virtue of forgiveness. He wouldn't be satisfied at all if he didn't get something suitable in return.

"Dammit! She's brazen. I'll make her mine.

"I'll get back to the breakup march later. First, she must be vanquished and transformed into a reserved, obedient, frugal woman who eats like a bird. The march will resume after the rebuke. The march cannot proceed because the way things are, it's too expensive.

"The secret of a contest is to get close to the enemy without the enemy knowing."

He found the address of Kinuko's apartment in the telephone directory. He bought a bottle of whiskey and two bags of peanuts. His ulterior motive was to feed her if she was hungry, then get her drunk with whiskey. He would pretend to be drunk and sleepy, and she would be his. Best of all, this was a bargain. There was no need to rent a room.

Something is very wrong when a man like Tajima who always brimmed with confidence regarding women to concoct this reckless, shameless, vulgar scheme. He may be going mad in his attempt to exploit Kinuko to this degree. Not only should lust be moderated, when people are particularly greedy and in a hurry to get their money's worth, it never ends well.

Tajima hated Kinuko so much, he devised this unworldly, petty, vulgar plan that, as expected, led to misfortune as serious as death.

That evening, Tajima found Kinuko's apartment in Setagaya. The apartment was in a dreary, old, two-story wooden building. Kinuko's room was right at the top of the stairs.

He knocked.

"Who is it?" called out that crow's voice from behind the door.

When the door opened, Tajima stood transfixed.

The mess. The stench.

It was bleak. The tatami mats covered a mere eighty square feet. Their surfaces were grimy and undulating, and not a trace of the edgings remained. The room was packed with the tools of the peddler's trade: oil cans, apple boxes, half-gallon bottles, other bundles wrapped by cloth, objects resembling bird cages, and scraps of paper. Everything was slimy and scattered about so there was almost no place to step.

"Oh, it's you. What are you doing here?"

Seeing Kinuko again in those clothes he recalled from several years ago, he felt that he could not tell whether this beggar wearing muddy Monpe pants was a man or a woman.

On one wall of the room hung an advertising poster of a credit finance company. None of the other walls was decorated. There weren't even any curtains. Is this the room of a twenty-five- or -six-year-old woman? A lone small light dimly lit the desolation.

9

SUPERHUMAN STRENGTH - 2

"I came to play," said Tajima overcome by horror then in a voice mimicking Kinuko's rasp said, "but maybe I'll come back some other time."

"You have an ulterior motive. You didn't just happen to be in this neighborhood."

"No, today, I actually..."

"Come on, come clean. You're a little too soft."

Nonetheless, that room was horrible.

Tajima thought, "Do we have to drink the whiskey here? Aah, I should have bought a cheaper brand."

"I'm not soft. I'm clean. You're dirtier than usual today, aren't you?" he asked disgusted.

"Today, I had to carry a load that was a bit heavy, so I'm beat. I'm gonna take a nap now. You've got some good stuff there. Why don't you rent a room? A cheap one."

She was talking about business. If making a profit were possible, the filth of that room was not a problem. Tajima took off his shoes and chose a relatively safe place on the tatami mats, and sat cross-legged, leaving his coat on.

"Do you like *karasumi*? We'll have it with our drinks," she said.

"Love it. You have some here? They'll be delicious."

"Cut it out. Give me some money."

Kinuko boldly pushed on the tip of Tajima's nose with the palm of her right hand.

Tajima twisted his mouth in disgust and said, "When I look at everything you do, life becomes futile. Please move your hand. I don't need any karasumi. It's horse food."

"But it's cheap, stupid. It's delicious because it's genuine. Stop messing around, give me the money."

Her body swayed, but she didn't pull back her hand.

Unfortunately, Tajima actually loved to eat karasumi along with whiskey. If he had that, he needed nothing else.

"A little more please?"

Annoyed, Tajima placed three large yen notes on the palm of Kinuko's hand.

"Four more," said Kinuko calmly.

A surprised Tajima said, "What! Come on!"

"A real tightwad. Be generous and buy one serving. I want to buy half a *katsuobushi*. You're so cheap."

"Okay, buy one serving."

The softie Tajima reached over, furious, and said, "Here, one, two, three, four. Is that enough? Take your hand away. I want to see the faces of the parents who gave birth to such a shameless person."

"I wanna see them, too. Then I wanna pretend to be a goody two-shoes. They say that even leeks wither and die when you throw them out."

"Your life story is dull. Give me a cup please. From now on, whiskey and karasumi...oh, and peanuts. I brought them for you."

10

SUPERHUMAN STRENGTH - 3

Tajima downed the large cup of whiskey in two gulps. Today, despite coming with the ulterior motive of rebuking Kinuko, he ended up buying some expensive genuine karasumi. And with no compunction, Kinuko crudely chopped up the whole serving of karasumi and piled it high in a dirty bowl, then sprinkled on a ton of imitation flavoring. She said, "Want some? The flavoring was free. It's okay if you don't want any."

So much of the karasumi was made inedible by the absurd amount of flavoring dumped on top. Tajima looked grief-stricken. Seven yen notes burned up by the fire of a candle. He could not remember ever feeling this intense loss. A true waste and meaningless.

Tajima felt like crying as he picked up and ate a sliver of karasumi not contaminated by the imitation flavoring at the bottom of the pile and timidly asked, "Do you cook?"

"I can, if I have to. But it's a pain, so I don't."

"Do you wash?"

"Don't be stupid. If I had my way, everything would be spotless."

"Spotless?"

Tajima was stupefied casting his eyes around the dreary, smelly room.

"This room has always been filthy. It's out of control. And my business is business. Anyhow, inside the room is different. You want to see? Look inside the closet," explained Kinuko.

He stood and opened the closet.

He looked inside.

A pure, orderly, golden light radiated out, and a pleasant fragrance was released. In addition to a dresser, there was a vanity table, a trunk, and three lovely small pairs of shoes on a shoebox. In other words, this closet was the secret backstage dressing room of a Cinderella princess with a crow's voice.

He immediately slammed the closet door shut. Sitting a short distance from Tajima, Kinuko said, "Is it stylish? It's enough for once a week. I don't think this room is particularly appealing to men, but for everyday clothes, this is perfect."

"But aren't those Monpe pants awful? They're unsanitary."

"Why?"

"They stink."

"I can't be prim and proper. Anyway, you always reek of liquor. A terrible stink."

"That makes us, partners in stink."

Accompanying his drunkenness, he became worried about the state of this bleak room and Kinuko's resemblance to a beggar. This instantly spawned the evil thought of trying to carry out his initial plan.

"We fight because we are close," he weakly argued. However, in this kind of situation, a man, even one said to be a great man or a great scholar, who foolishly flirts like this will succeed beyond expectation.

11

SUPERHUMAN STRENGTH - 4

"I hear a piano," he said to show off a bit.

He narrowed his eyes and tilted his ear toward a distant radio.

"You know about music, too? You look like you're tone deaf," she said.

"Idiot. You may not realize it, but I'm a bit of an authority on music. I could listen to great works all day, everyday."

"What's that playing?"

He randomly tossed out, "Chopin."

"Really? I thought it was *Echigo Lion*."

This was the absurd conversation of a tone-deaf duo. Since neither of them livened up, Tajima hurriedly switched topics.

"Have you ever been in love?"

"What is wrong with you? Definitely not to a lecher like you."

"Why don't you watch what you say? You tramp."

Tajima immediately tensed up and gulped down some more whiskey. He may have already failed. But to retreat now would reflect on his reputation as a ladies' man. He was determined to succeed at all costs.

"Love and lust are fundamentally different. You don't know a thing. Let me teach you, okay?"

He recalled feeling a chill at his disagreeable tone as he spoke. That was no good. Although it was a little early, he would pretend to be drunk and sleepy.

"Aaah, I'm drunk. I drank too much on an empty stomach. Can I sleep here?"

"No!"

That crow's voice was more jarring.

"I'm not stupid. I see what you're up to. If you want to stay, you can pay me half a million, no a million yen."

It was a catastrophic failure.

"No need to get so mad. I'm drunk, so this is..."

"No! No! No! Go home!"

Kinuko stood up and opened the door.

On the spot, Tajima devised the most inept, clumsy plan. He quickly stood and tried to embrace Kinuko.

Pow! His cheek met her fist. Tajima let out a loud, unworldly howl. At that moment, he recalled the superhuman strength possessed by Kinuko who effortlessly carried eighty pounds and shuddered.

"Please forgive me. Thief!" he cried for some odd reason and dashed out into the hallway, barefoot.

Kinuko calmly closed the door.

A few moments later, outside the door, he said, "Um...excuse me...sorry...but...my shoes...and a string or something like that, please...the temples of my glasses broke."

While he registered the seething in his guts of never having been so thoroughly humiliated in his history as a ladies' man, he used the red tape kindly bestowed on him by Kinuko to repair his glasses and hang the temples over both ears, and said, "Thank you!"

He was crying in despair as he descended the stairs, and punctuated his crying with a squeal when he missed a step.

12

THE COLD WAR - 1

However, Tajima did not regret the capital invested in Nagai Kinuko. This was not a business with no gain. He used her, and to say he didn't get his money's worth would be a lie. But that superhuman strength, that huge appetite, and that greed.

It was getting warmer and a variety of flowers was beginning to bloom, but only Tajima was deeply depressed. Four or five days had passed since the fiasco the other night. But he had a brand new pair of glasses, and the swelling in his cheek had gone down, so he called Kinuko's apartment. He thought about first employing ideological warfare.

"Hello. It's Tajima. I got too drunk the other day. Ha, ha, ha."

"I'm a single woman. Things happen. Don't worry about it."

"No, I've been thinking a lot since then and have come to this conclusion. I was going to break up with those women, buy a small house, send for my wife and child in the country, and make a happy home, but is this morally wrong?"

"What are you talking about? You're not making sense. Any man with a boatload of money would come up with that kind of miserly plan."

"That's why it's bad."

"Well, it's not good. Haven't you saved up a lot?"

"I'm not just talking about money...morality, that is, the problem is ideological. What do you think?"

"I don't think anything. What's wrong with you?"

"That's natural, but I think this is good."

"Well then, it is good. I'm hanging up. This call is a waste."

"But this is a problem of life and death for me. I think that I must respect morality. Please help me. Help me. I want to do the right thing."

"You're a strange one. You're probably pretending to be drunk again so you can act like a fool. How sad."

"This isn't a joke. Everyone has the instinct to do good."

"Can I hang up? Is there anything else? Listen, I really got to pee. I'm hopping up and down here."

"Wait, give me a few more seconds. 3,000 yen a day."

The ideological warfare suddenly turned to talk of money.

"With meals?"

"No. Please help. I'm not making much these days."

"No deal for less than 10,000 yen."

"How about 5,000 yen? Please. This is an issue of morality."

"I gotta pee. I've been patient."

"Then it's 5,000 yen."

"You jerk!"

He heard her stifle a laugh, the sign of an agreement.

13

THE COLD WAR - 2

At 5,000 yen a day, he would have to use Kinuko to the fullest. If he treated her to anything, even a scrap of bread or a glass of water, and didn't exploit her as much as possible, he wouldn't profit. Consideration was forbidden, it would ruin him.

Although he let out that unworldly howl when slugged by Kinuko, Tajima had found a way to use her superhuman strength.

One of his lovers was Mizuhara Keiko. She was just shy of thirty years old and a fairly poor oil painter. She rented a two-room apartment in Denencho-shi. One room was her living room and the other, her studio. Mizuhara-san had a letter of introduction from some painter. Tajima found her timidity to be cute as she blushed while asking to do illustrations, woodcuts, or any artwork for *Obelisk*, so he helped a bit with her living expenses. She was quiet and had a gentle demeanor, but she was a big crybaby. However, it was not that crazed, baying, unladylike crying. Her crying was not so bad, it was sweet like a little girl's.

Nevertheless, she had a major flaw, an older brother. He had been stationed in Manchuria for a long time and had been a thug since childhood. He was very masculine with a solid physique. Ever since Keiko first spoke of him, Tajima had been troubled. Since the days of Faust, a man like this sergeant or corporal older brother of a woman has been a menacing presence to her lover.

Recently, this brother had returned from Siberia and was toughing it out in Keiko's living room.

Tajima had no interest in meeting this brother. When he called the apartment to extract her, he failed.

"I'm Keiko's brother...," said her strong brother in a powerful voice. It was as Tajima had expected.

His voice quivering, Tajima said, "I'm calling from the magazine. I'd like to discuss a drawing assignment with..."

"She can't do anything. She has a cold and is sleeping. She can't work now."

What bad luck. He was unable to extract Keiko.

However, it seemed to him that he was being rude to Keiko by hesitating to break up with her out of fear of her brother. Now, with Keiko down with a cold and living with her repatriated brother, money would definitely be a problem. On the other hand, this may be his chance. He would visit her in her sickbed to express his concern and quietly slip her money. Then her soldier brother probably wouldn't hit him. Or he would probably be more moved than Keiko and seek to shake hands. In the rare event, violence were directed at Tajima...at that time...he could hide behind the superhuman strength of Nagai Kuniko.

One hundred percent of her would be put to use.

"Good? I think it will be okay. There will be only one violent man present. If he raises his hand, you will gently take him down. He seems to be a weakling."

He spoke to Kinuko with remarkable politeness.

[TRANSLATOR'S NOTE: This story was never finished. The author Dazai Osamu committed suicide with his lover Yamazaki Tomie on June 13, 1948.]

CREDITS

Pandora's Box

Cover Image:
John William Waterhouse, Public domain, via Wikimedia Commons
https://commons.wikimedia.org/wiki/File:
John_William_Waterhouse_-_Pandora,_1896.jpg

Dazai's silhouette derived from:
Unknown authorUnknown author, Public domain, via Wikimedia Commons
https://commons.wikimedia.org/wiki/File:OsamuDazai.jpg

Japanese Source Text:
Originally serialized in *Kahoku Shinpo*, Kahoku Shinpo-sha, October 22, 1945 to January 7, 1946.
Aozora Bunko
http://www.aozora.gr.jp/cards/000035/card1566.html

Translation of Issa's dewdrop world poem:
Lewis Mackenzie

http://en.wikipedia.org/wiki/Kobayashi_Issa

Goodbye

Prologue:
Republished in "Mono Omou Ashi," *Shincho Bunko*, Shincho Co.,
September 25, 1980.
太宰治、「グッド ·バイ」作者の言葉、
http://www.aozora.gr.jp/cards/000035/card42357.html

Japanese Source Text:
Originally published in *Asahi Hyouron*, July 1948.
太宰治、 グッド・バイ 、
http://www.aozora.gr.jp/cards/000035/card258.html

ABOUT THE AUTHOR

Dazai Osamu (1909-1948) was a major 20th-century Japanese author of fiction. His most popular novels were *The Setting Sun* and *No Longer Human*.